DONORS, DECEPTION & DEATH

A Dogwood Springs Cozy Mystery

SALLY BAYLESS

Kimberlin Belle Publishing

Copyright © 2023 by Sally Bayless

All rights reserved. This book or any portion thereof may not be reproduced or used in any manner whatsoever without the express written permission of the publisher except for the use of brief quotations in a book review.

ISBN: 978-1-946034-29-8

Kimberlin Belle Publishing

Contact: admin@kimberlinbelle.com

Publisher's Note: This is a work of fiction. Names, characters, places, and incidents are a product of the author's imagination. Locales and public names are sometimes used for atmospheric purposes. Any resemblance to actual people, living or dead, or to businesses, companies, events, institutions, or locales is completely coincidental.

Cover art by DLR Cover Designs, www.dlrcoverdesigns.com.

Chapter One

Friday, February 23

"THIS UPCOMING DONOR reception might be the death of me." I looked up, swallowed back my dread, and once again started climbing the ladder.

As director of the Dogwood Springs History Museum, much of my job was fundraising, but the gift we were preparing to recognize at the reception had come as a complete surprise. I'd been pulling the event together amid hosting four school groups that had arranged months ago to visit the museum.

Whenever I had a snippet of time, I worked on a PowerPoint presentation about what the donor's gift would mean for the museum, polished a press release to send out the day after the reception, or called to confirm details like the rented tables, chairs, and linens. Of course, I was incredibly grateful for the gift, but if I had to deal with one more special request from the donor's wife—

"What is this, Libby, your fourth attempt to get these curtains rehung?" Alice VanMeter, who was holding the ladder, gestured to the teal, floor-to-ceiling draperies. Alice, the president of the museum's board and its number one volunteer, had been invaluable over the past week.

"Fifth. I thought we had it last time, but that bulge at the top left makes me think one of the curtain hooks is loose."

Back when the museum had been built as a private home in 1920, the room we were in had been an upstairs den. It was a nice size, and it had a lovely historic fireplace and large, tall windows.

When my staff and I cleaned out the room in preparation for the reception, we got rid of dozens of outdated displays, as well as boxes of useless files from the 1970s.

In the process of hauling one of those boxes, I bumped into the curtains. Dust billowed out and dead spiders rained down. Dead spiders were, of course, better than live ones, which really, really gave me the creeps, but dry cleaning those curtains had been essential. As old as they were, we were lucky they hadn't disintegrated.

Unfortunately, taking down those curtains was a lot easier than putting them back up, especially because this room, like all the rooms on the second floor of the museum, had twelve-foot ceilings.

I went up another step on the wooden ladder, and it creaked.

I froze for a second, but the ladder seemed fine.

A blurry image of my pale face and dark hair reflected back at me in the window. I looked past it, at the cold, dreary day outside. It was getting dark, and we needed to get this finished. Besides, I was almost there.

I climbed a step higher, up past the point where I felt comfortable. Really, this was not what I'd envisioned when I'd chosen a career working in museums.

But being the director of a small-town history museum in southern Missouri involved all sorts of unusual tasks, a few of them unpleasant. Those were tasks I was willing to do, though, if it meant the museum would receive a large check from a donor. After all, it was my name, Libby Ballard, that was listed on the museum's website as the director.

And as a director who'd been at the museum less than a year, a director trying to rebuild her life at age thirty-three after going through an ugly divorce and having her previous museum position sabotaged by her ex-husband, I was doubly motivated to make this job a success.

Finally, I was high enough on the ladder. I clutched the side rail with one hand and stretched my other arm up, reaching for the top of the teal velvet curtain so I could release the hooks between the loose one and the edge of the panel. There was no way to fix one hook in the middle. I had to go back to the problem and work my way out and—

A scream reverberated through the second floor.

I jerked back.

The ladder wobbled.

My heart raced, and I squawked out a weak yelp as I tried to climb down. If I fell, the curtains would be the least of my worries.

"I've got you," Alice yelled.

The ladder stopped moving.

"I'm so sorry," she said. "That scream distracted me, and I let go."

"Thank you for recovering so quickly." I clung to the side rails of the ladder, gasping for breath. Still shaky, I made my way back to the floor. "But what on earth is going on?"

"It sounded like Imani, but are you sure you're all right?" Alice's brown eyes narrowed, and she looked me up and down.

"I'm fine, because of you." I held my arms out, displaying that I was uninjured.

"Thank goodness." Alice rested a hand on my shoulder.

Although the stylish cut of her chin-length brown hair made her appear younger, Alice was fifty-six, old enough to be my mom. One of the most nurturing people I'd ever known, she was not only vital to the museum, she was also a dear friend. Simply hearing the caring in her voice helped slow my heart rate back to normal.

"We'd better check on Imani," I said. "I hope she didn't get a call saying there was something wrong with the baby." Imani Jones, the museum's education coordinator, had only returned from maternity leave two weeks ago. Little Laila was three months old and, without question, the cutest baby I'd ever seen.

"Laila's fine," Imani said as she walked in from the hall. "Sorry I screamed. I just got so frustrated." She shoved her Bluetooth earbuds into the pocket of her vintage sixties avocado green minidress. "The baby was up for hours last night, and I'm running on fumes."

If I had to guess, I'd say Imani had been listening to music, and had no idea that her cry almost made me fall.

She planted her hands on her hips. "The problem—once again—is the current Mrs. Cordell Calhoun."

I rolled my eyes. Her again. No wonder Imani was upset. Brittany Calhoun was the worst potential donor, or spouse of a potential donor, I'd encountered in a decade of museum work. "What does Brittany want now?"

"She's started a new 'health regimen.'" Imani put air quotes around the words, then drew her box braids together with both hands and pulled them over one shoulder. "She emailed and changed her menu request for the third time in less than a week. Now she says she wants a vegan meal." Imani's long eyelashes brushed her cheeks as she closed her eyes for a moment and drew in a deep breath. "The caterer is going to have a fit. Just yesterday, they were finally able to source the ethically raised specialty fish she wanted."

"Oh, brother." I wasn't sure how much more of this woman the museum could take. Brittany, the third wife of Cordell Calhoun, the donor we were honoring, created new problems almost daily for the reception we were planning.

"Cordell is an idiot." Rodney Grant, the museum's curator, carried in a cardboard box and set it on one of the round tables the rental company had delivered yesterday. "I brought up the rest of those centerpieces, Alice."

Rodney, who was in his early sixties, had a knee replacement done last August. It had taken a while to get his mobility back, but these days, he seemed to delight in what he referred to as his new lease on life, always looking for another way to be active.

Though the rest of us had only recently met Cordell and Brittany, Rodney was, in a way, related to them. His older sister had been Cordell's first wife.

He shook his head, and the light glinted off his gray hair. "The man made his money selling spicy fried chicken and extra-flaky biscuits. What was he thinking, marrying a woman who won't eat meat or carbs?"

"What was he thinking?" Imani let out an unladylike snort. "Brittany is twenty-eight, gorgeous, and built like a Barbie doll. The man's about to celebrate his seventieth birthday, and they've been married, what, a year? There was no thinking involved when he proposed."

I had to agree. If I thought too long about the fact that Cordell had married a woman young enough to be his granddaughter, it made my skin crawl. And Brittany was the poster girl for the phrase Trophy Wife. As well as a few other less polite phrases.

I turned to Imani. "Beg if you must when you talk to the caterer. One way or another, we need everybody happy at this reception." Cordell's donation would take the museum's capital campaign past the goal for a much-needed elevator, and it would fund the remodeling of the room we were standing in, a large space on the second floor we'd be able to use for a display area once the elevator allowed accessibility.

When we learned that Cordell planned to celebrate his seventieth birthday by donating to several organizations in Dogwood Springs, one of them the museum, we'd made plans to hold a reception here in his honor.

"I still say this event would have been easier if we'd held it at La Villetta," Rodney said.

"It would have," I agreed. "But the mayor worked out an events schedule for all the organizations receiving donations. As the smallest group, we got Monday night, when La Villetta is closed." I was grateful I'd found a caterer who was available. Dogwood Springs had several upscale restaurants up and down Main Street, but only La Villetta had a separate room for private events.

"Well, at least I got the seating chart figured out," Alice said.

"Thank you." Once again, Alice was a lifesaver.

"Happy to help," she said. "But Cordell's insistence that his current wife, his two ex-wives, his children, and his adult grandson all attend the reception made seating arrangements a little tricky."

"I'm telling you, this whole week is a bad idea." Rodney's lips thinned.

I went back up the ladder, this time with Alice firmly holding the base. "The mayor said that every time Cordell is honored during his birthday week here in Dogwood Springs, the family is expected to be in attendance."

Not my idea of fun, but when the family patriarch was the king of a fried chicken empire that included more than three thousand fast-food restaurants nationwide, people tended to go along with his plans. "The only event that's optional is the last day, March 1, the opening day of trout season, when Cordell plans to go fishing."

"I only saw the entire family together once before, when Cordell's mother died," Rodney said. "People walked around like the cemetery had been planted with land mines, trying to avoid each other."

I fixed the loose curtain hook, climbed back down, and gave the window a nod of approval. One thing, at least, was within my control.

"My sister and Cordell's second wife hate each other, and they've passed that animosity along to their offspring," Rodney explained. "The only thing they agree on is that they both hate Brittany even more."

"I'm glad you told me all that before I did the seating chart," Alice said. "I've got three tables, six chairs at each, and I had to fit in eight members of the family, including Cordell and Brittany. I tried to mix people up more, but I finally put each branch of the family at its own table, then filled in with members of the museum board and city council."

"Where am I?" Imani asked.

Alice walked to her purse, which was sitting on a nearby table, pulled out a sheet of paper, and pointed to it. "You're here, with Cordell's second wife and her family. And Rodney, you're here, with your sister." She turned to me.

"The head table is you, me, the mayor, the city council president, Cordell, and Brittany."

I found my name on the seating chart. Oh, goody. A whole meal sitting by Brittany.

After a cocktail hour where the entire group of eighteen —including Brittany and six family members who hated her —was supposed to chat amiably.

What could possibly go wrong?

Chapter Two

"TELL CLEO that I hope her ankle gets better soon." Marcus, the owner of the Dogwood Café, handed me my order when I popped in a half hour later.

"I will." I slid on my gloves and picked up my umbrella and the to-go order, soaking in one last bit of warmth before I left the cozy café and stepped back out onto Main Street.

I walked quickly through downtown, dodging well-bundled tourists, eager to get home after staying late on a Friday at the museum. Even on a damp, chilly day in late February—a day when it was too warm to snow and too cold to be comfortable—I loved Dogwood Springs.

At first, when I'd taken the job here last summer, I had my doubts. Oh, I believed that everyone should have access to history so they could see how interesting it was. And I believed having that access could make a tangible difference in people's lives. But I was used to living in a big city and working in a large, prestigious historic house museum. The

Dogwood Springs History Museum hadn't been my first, second, or even my fourteenth choice of a place to work. To my surprise, I found real purpose here, as well as wonderful people. Even if a top-tier museum called out of the blue and offered me a job, I'd say no. Dogwood Springs was the place for me.

It certainly didn't hurt that the town offered darling shops, a local winery, a three-story library, and far more upscale restaurants than any other small town I knew.

Besides, the place was downright charming.

Colorful awnings lined the street, protecting the entrances to the shops and restaurants from spring showers. Pots of purple and yellow pansies sat beside each door. And a smorgasbord of heavenly aromas floated out of the businesses as I headed home—the scent of fresh baked bread from La Villetta, the aroma of peanut butter cookies from the bakery, and the fragrance of deep, rich chocolate from the candy shop.

It was hard not to detour into Mimi's Candies, but I had dinner to deliver.

Before long, I turned onto Elm Street and, through the bare branches of the maples that lined the street, saw my home. My apartment was the first floor of a plain, two-story white frame house built in 1900. It was nothing fancy, but it fit my budget, was a fifteen-minute walk from the museum, and had a few elements, like the original, hand-carved mantel, that delighted the historian in me. But what really made it home was Bella, my golden retriever, and Cleo, my upstairs neighbor and best friend.

I went in through the front door, which led to a small, shared entryway, called upstairs to Cleo to let her know I'd be up soon, and opened the door to my apartment.

Bella was right there to greet me. She let out a woof and circled me, tail wagging, brown eyes bright and full of love.

"One second, girl." I set my big purse on a chair and the to-go bag on my dining table and bent down to say hello.

She licked my cheek and gazed up at me, eager for attention.

My heart filled with love. "I missed you too." Bella was such a joy in my life. I petted her back, rubbed the soft fur between her ears, and then took her out to the backyard. Barely a day went by when I didn't reflect that adopting her had been one of the best decisions of my life.

A few minutes later, we returned to the kitchen, where Bella stared pointedly at the cabinet where I stored the dog food.

I filled her bowl with dry food, added her favorite canned food on top, and refilled her water bowl. "You go ahead and eat, girl. I need to check on Cleo."

Bella needed no encouragement and began to wolf down her dinner. When I adopted her, I'd quickly been impressed with how well trained she was. Eating slowly, however, must not have been part of doggy manners training.

And, of course, there was the occasional issue, like a couple of nights ago when I took her to the office with me after the museum closed. I had wanted to finish up the slides for my presentation at the reception and thought she could sit happily in my office. Instead, she'd slipped downstairs when I wasn't looking and chewed on a man's boot in a display of life in the Victorian era.

Luckily, I realized she was gone and stopped her before she did much harm. I showed the damage to Rodney, and he said the tooth marks didn't look that much different from normal wear on the other boot. I apologized profusely and had a talk with Bella about the issue.

But now it was time to take Cleo her dinner. I changed into warm, fuzzy slippers, grabbed the to-go bag from the café, and went back out to the foot of the stairs in the entryway. "Ready for a visitor?" I called up the stairs.

"Yes!" Cleo's voice rang down.

Upstairs, the door to Cleo's apartment was open. I walked in and found her sitting on the couch, back against the armrest, legs stretched out on the cushions. One ankle was wrapped in a compression bandage and propped on a pillow.

"Marcus at the café heard about your accident. He sent you a free piece of chocolate cream pie to go with your meal. Do you want to eat now?" I raised the carryout bag.

Behind her oversized glasses, Cleo's brown eyes lit. "Ooh! Chocolate pie from the Dogwood Café! Thank you, Marcus, and thank you, Libby. I'm not really hungry yet, though. Still full from when Mom was here at lunch." She gestured toward her kitchen. "Would you mind sticking it in the fridge?"

"Happy to." I stepped into Cleo's kitchen, struck once

again by how our two apartments matched our personalities.

Downstairs, my place was decorated with antiques and fabrics in soft blues and tans, creating a soothing, peaceful oasis. Upstairs, Cleo's place featured vivid lime and cobalt, dramatic artwork, and small explosions of accent colors.

While I was logical and organized, Cleo was creative, spontaneous, and sometimes a little loud. And, even though I'd known her less than a year, she was also the best friend I'd ever had. From the day we met, she'd welcomed me and helped me feel like Dogwood Springs was my home.

I tucked the carryout bag into Cleo's fridge next to a bottle of salsa, a half-gallon of milk, and a clear container of what looked like homemade soup. That had to be Cleo's mom's doing. The only thing Cleo ever made from scratch was guacamole.

"How are you?" I asked as I came back into the living room. "And what did the doctor say about your ankle?"

"It's a sprain." Cleo ran a hand through her short blond pixie cut. "I have to stay completely off it for two days, and if I do a good job with ice, rest, the bandage, and keeping it elevated, I should be able to go back to work next week." Cleo folded her arms over her chest. "I tried to tell the doctor that I run a hair salon, that my clients need me, but she said if I don't let it heal, I could be dealing with problems for a lot longer."

"I'm glad it's not broken." I pictured the conversation between Cleo and the doctor. Thankfully, Cleo's mom lived across town and had taken her to the clinic to be checked out. If I had to guess, her mom knew that it would take a doctor's orders to make Cleo slow down. Her high energy was great for running her own business, but bad for sitting still.

Cleo adjusted the hot pink pillow under her leg. "That new stylist I hired is going to be working a lot of extra hours this week, whether she likes it or not. We had to totally rearrange the schedule. And I assure you, she got an earful about the fact that leaving a perm roller on the floor could lead to someone getting injured." Cleo moved the pillow again and winced.

"Do you need me to bring you ice? Are you in pain?"

"No. I'm fine if I just lie here. But I'm soooooo bored." Cleo held up her phone. "I've spent the entire day doing the same craft project, looking at social media, and watching TV. But now that you're home, we can open the package."

"What package?" I glanced around her apartment. I spotted the craft project in process—something that involved piles of brightly colored netting—but no unopened package.

"It's the dress! My mom brought the package in from the porch so it wouldn't get wet and read the label. It's downstairs in the entryway, right by the door to your apartment."

"I guess I missed it." I stood. "I'll go get it and bring it up so you can see it."

"And so you can try it on," Cleo said.

Or not. But at least she could see me hold it up.

I went down the stairs and found the box by my door. I guess I'd been so glad to be home that I hadn't noticed it.

Sure enough, the return address was the clothing company that Cleo had persuaded me to order a dress from.

Ordinarily, I'd never have considered it, preferring clothing that was more conservative. But after the way Cleo had changed my hair from a straight, dark brown that hung on each side of my face to a slightly lighter shade that flattered my complexion and gave me a cut that brushed my shoulders and moved gracefully, I valued her opinion.

At least enough to order the dress.

I stuck my head into my apartment. "Bella, do you want to come up and see Cleo?"

Bella rose from where she was stretched out on the rug in front of the fireplace, gave a quick shake that made her tags jingle, and trotted over to me.

"We have to be very careful of Cleo's ankle," I said. "She's hurt."

Bella tipped her head as if she understood.

I wouldn't be surprised if she did.

More and more, since I moved to Dogwood Springs eight months ago and adopted her, I'd come to realize how smart Bella was.

We climbed the stairs, and Bella went over to Cleo, waited for her to pet her, and laid down in front of the couch as if guarding her.

"Well, what's taking so long?" Cleo said. "Rip it open and try it on."

I got a table knife from the kitchen and carefully cut through the tape. I wasn't ripping anything. There was a good chance this dress was going back. A very good chance, given what I remembered of the style. "I'll open it, but I don't want to try it on right now."

"Why not?" Cleo looked at me like I'd turned down homemade shortbread cookies, my favorite. "It's going to look fabulous, and it will be perfect for that fancy dinner with Sam you're so worried about."

"It might." On the other hand, it might look cheap and tacky and expose far too much cleavage for a formal event at Grove University.

It had taken a while, but I'd gotten used to the fact that Sam Collins, the man I was dating, had made millions in tech in California. He didn't flaunt his wealth, and most of the time, he seemed like an ordinary person.

After he left industry, though, to keep himself busy, he'd taken a job teaching computer science at the local college, a job that allowed him to be closer to his family in St. Louis.

Recently, he'd invited me to a dinner where he was receiving a teaching award. I'd have to make conversation with a room full of tenured faculty, people who had Ph.D.'s and long strings of other initials after their names.

Sam and I had run into one of his colleagues at the grocery store once. I could honestly say that the only words I understood from their conversation were hello, software, and coding.

Of course, in my own field, I was knowledgeable. I had a master's degree in public history. And although I wasn't extremely extroverted, I was good with people. After all, fundraising was a big part of my job. Worst-case scenario, if I was stuck in a conversation with one of Sam's colleagues, I could always ask about their research, and—when I was totally clueless—smile and nod.

Even so, this event had me stressed. It wasn't really the prospect of talking to all those academics. It was the fact that attending a formal awards ceremony at Grove University with Sam moved our relationship to a higher level of commitment. I would be meeting his colleagues, and almost every other couple there would be married.

Don't get me wrong. I liked Sam a lot. But because of my divorce, finalized only fourteen months ago, I was still somewhat cautious in our relationship.

With all that emotional baggage packed for the evening, would wearing a dress that was inappropriate help?

Hardly.

But I might as well take a peek. I slid the dress out of its plastic bag.

"Finally. Hold it up so I can see." Cleo gestured with one hand to hurry me along.

I lifted the dress by the shoulders.

"The color is exactly like it was pictured," Cleo exclaimed. "And look at that fabric!"

"It's very soft." I rubbed it between my fingers, then handed the dress to Cleo so she could appreciate it. The material was a silky, finely woven polyester with a bit of stretch in a dark emerald shade. If the dress happened to fit well, the color would bring out my green eyes, my best feature.

I still had my doubts about the style. The dress had elbow-length sleeves, a deep V in the back, and a wrap-style front with a slightly shallower V-neck. It gathered at the waist and was floor length, with a high slit up one leg.

I took a long look at the neckline and the slit up the leg. "I think the dress would probably be fine on someone taller, like you, but I'm barely five-feet-five. Don't you think it's a bit much?"

"Absolutely not. Go put it on."

"Oh, I don't want to now." Later, alone in my apartment was a far better plan.

"Seriously? I've been here bored all day, and I'm injured and in pain, and you would deny me this small bit of joy?" Cleo widened her eyes.

I crossed my arms and raised one eyebrow. "You already said you're not in pain."

"Maybe not physical pain, but emotional pain. The injury, being here alone all day..."

I knew for a fact that her mom had stayed for several hours.

Cleo held the dress toward me and let out a huge sigh.

Never let it be said that my best friend wasn't dramatic.

I raised my hands in surrender and took the dress into Cleo's bedroom.

A minute later, I looked at myself in her full-length mirror, and a hollow tingle filled my chest.

The dress was not bad. Not bad at all. The V-neck in the front wasn't nearly as low-cut once it was on. And the dress seemed to have been designed by some fashion genius so that it hugged in the right places and had extra room exactly where a woman might need it. I took one last glance in the mirror and walked out into the living room.

Cleo burst out clapping. "Fabulous! Turn around."

I slowly spun.

"You're going to knock them dead." She beamed. "Look at you. You're already standing taller. If there's one thing I know as a stylist, it's that looking good can give someone a boost of self-confidence. That fancy awards dinner at the university sounds more appealing, doesn't it?"

"Yeah," I said. "I have to admit it does."

The dress was too formal for the donor reception at the museum on Monday, and the university awards dinner was only two days later, on Wednesday night. But if this new dress wasn't quite so fancy, and if I had time for dry cleaning, I'd probably wear it to the donor reception as well, instead of the black dress I had planned to wear.

After all, Cordell Calhoun's donation was crucial for my plan to add an elevator and expand the museum's display space. Some extra confidence would be welcome if I was going to make that reception run flawlessly.

Chapter Three

WHEN THE DONOR reception started Monday night, I'd had plenty of time to think about the Calhoun family dynamic. Enough time that simply looking at the rented tables covered in white tablecloths and hearing the murmur of conversation made my stomach tense.

I had my doubts that Cordell's family could make it through the various events of the entire week without some sort of blowup. By the time they attended the events for Cordell's donation to the library or the local football team at the end of the week, I imagined even the concerted efforts of the event organizers would fall short. But maybe, just maybe, we could make it through tonight's event without a crisis, especially since I'd come up with a plan.

Once the family members sat down for dinner according to Alice's seating chart, the three branches of the family should be peacefully divided. During the cocktail hour, my staff and the museum board members would run interference, keeping pleasant, happy topics flowing.

Luckily, Rodney had filled us in on details about the various family members, and they were easy to tell apart by hair color.

Rodney's sister, Paula Calhoun, was Cordell's first wife. She was seventy and had short white hair that had once been blond. Her daughter, Heather, and grandson, Emmett, had inherited her fair hair.

I wandered over near Paula and Heather, who were chatting in the northwest corner of the room.

Paula wore chocolate brown pants, a dressy green-and-brown top, and tortoiseshell-frame glasses. She had a no-nonsense attitude about her that matched her sensible brown flats. In contrast, fifty-year-old Heather wore three-inch heels and a ruffled, pale pink dress scattered with huge, dark pink flowers. The dress was too snug, drawing attention to her weight, and, in my opinion, the fabric looked like a wallpaper pattern that should have been discontinued.

"I see no reason to pretend. I hate that little gold digger." Paula muttered to Heather as she added another slice of cheese and a fancy cracker to her appetizer plate.

I glanced around until I made sure Brittany was on the far side of the room and then, so it wouldn't seem like I was eavesdropping, looked out the window and pretended to watch the occasional flake of snow that drifted down in the moonlight.

What did I know about Paula? Because it was time to

start a conversation with her and redirect her thoughts in a more positive, convivial direction.

Thanks to Rodney, I knew that she was a retired pharmacist, had been in Cordell's class in the Dogwood Springs schools, and was his high school sweetheart. Perhaps I could ask her what Cordell was like in high school?

"Mo-m." Heather drew the word out into two long, disapproving syllables as she brushed a spot of dirt off her dress. She lowered her voice, but I could still hear every word. "I know this week is a trial, but Daddy has enough money to leave each of us a seven-figure inheritance. If you don't want the money yourself, at least be on your best behavior for me." She laid a hand over her chest. "I, for one, don't want to be written out of the will."

According to Rodney, Heather was a wonderful occupational therapist, who was beloved by her patients and co-workers alike. And, although she didn't know it, by keeping her mother in line, she was serving a vital role in my plan for a peaceful reception.

I didn't see Emmett, Heather's twenty-five-year-old son, but perhaps he had slipped out to use the restroom. For now, the first branch of the family appeared to be under control.

Rodney and the mayor had just filled their plates at the appetizer table and were walking toward Paula and Heather. Maria Wilder, a young museum board member who owned the winery that produced the wines we were serving, was moving toward them as well, with a bottle of white in one hand and a bottle of red in the other. She winked at me, and I knew that corner of the room wouldn't be a problem.

I made my way over to where the second branch of Cordell's family was clustered in another corner of the room.

Cordell's second wife, Leah, had dark hair that fell almost to her shoulders, dark eyes, a February tan that hinted at tropical vacations, and a tall, lean figure that looked as if she worked out a lot. According to Rodney, she had been Cordell's secretary before they married.

Leah's two sons, Brad and Nick Calhoun, were both tall and dark haired, like their mom. Brad, the older son, was thirty-three, clean-shaven with short hair, and looked every inch the businessman. His younger brother, Nick, was twenty-nine, had wavy, shoulder-length hair, a beard and mustache, and a sexy, earthy vibe that fit his profession as a potter.

Imani and Mortimer Townsend, a dean at Grove University and museum board member, were deep in conversation with the three of them.

I walked up next to Imani. "Is everything going well?"

Everyone responded in the affirmative, and Mortimer gave me a slow nod that said there was no need for worry. From what Sam had said about the egos at Grove University, Mortimer probably dealt with situations a lot trickier than this on a regular basis.

I stayed a moment longer, laughed at a not-very-funny joke from Brad, and excused myself, saying I needed to chat with all the guests.

Time for me to move over near the fireplace, to check on Cordell and Brittany, who were talking with Alice and the head of the Dogwood Springs city council.

I greeted them and listened to Cordell describe the classic Mustangs he'd been collecting for the past twenty-five years, then tell about his last big fishing trip. A short, jovial man with white hair and a pudgy nose, Cordell was a good storyteller, and there was an air about him that said that he'd made sure to enjoy himself along the path to success.

Nick, Leah's younger son, the potter, wandered up to hear the fishing story, smiling at both his dad and Brittany. Good for Nick. At least one member of the family could be civil to the third wife.

The councilman, Nick, and Alice all acted interested in Cordell's fishing story, and the councilman even asked a question about bait that kept Cordell engaged. But Brittany ignored her husband completely, scanning the room and looking bored.

I forced myself to give her a friendly smile. Frankly, even if we hadn't been dealing with her frustrating phone calls all week, I'd have found Brittany off-putting. Not only was she rude to her husband, but the woman was flashy in a way that bugged me.

She had red hair that may or may not have been natural, flawless skin, and big, pouty lips that she'd painted a rich coral. Although it was a chilly night and the invitation had said business casual, she wore a sleeveless pale aqua cocktail dress that looked like it had been sprayed on. And, in contrast with the business-appropriate black dress and family pearls I was wearing, Brittany's dress showed not just a hint of her disproportionately ample cleavage but gave a blatant invitation to what was barely covered.

Cordell finished his story and glanced over at Brittany, his eyes lingering only briefly on that cleavage as he hooked an arm around her waist. "Isn't that right, honeybun?"

"Absolutely," she said. Like a switch, she flipped off the bored expression and gave him an attentive smile. A smile that oozed fakeness, but one that made his eyes light up in response.

"Maybe I should visit the buffet table, see if they have any more of those fried chicken tenders." Cordell started toward the appetizers, then stopped. "Well, now, I guess everyone here loves fried chicken as much as I do. Those tenders are all gone. I'll have to wait for the main course, I guess."

What? I'd made a special point of telling the caterer to keep the chicken tenders piled high.

"Where do you plan to fish on the opening day of trout season, Cordell?" Alice said.

Thank you, Alice. I excused myself, hurried to the hall, and headed down the back staircase toward the conference room where the caterer was staging the food.

Halfway down the stairs, I met one of the catering staff, a girl carrying a large tray. "Tell me that's more chicken tenders."

"It is." The girl's cheeks turned almost as pink as the streak in her tight blond bun. "Sorry for the delay."

I exhaled. "No worries. Get those upstairs right away and, once you have them on the table, put a few on a plate and offer it to the older man with white hair in the light gray suit."

"Will do."

I pressed my body against the wall, and the server slid past me with the precious tray of chicken.

When I reached the top of the stairs, one of the city council members told me about a stopped-up toilet in the ladies' room. By the time I plunged it and thoroughly washed my hands, the chicken supply had been replenished. Cordell had left his empty wine glass by his chair and was focused on food. He had a plate of tenders in his hand and stood by the appetizers, spooning honey mustard—his personal favorite, which we'd made sure was on the menu—onto his plate. Brittany was in front of the fireplace near the head table, tossing back a long drink of red wine.

Whew. All was well. Finally, the knot in my stomach eased. Only ten more minutes of cocktail hour, and then I could ask everyone to take their seats. I snagged a chicken tender and ate it.

And then, like some kind of horror film, Brittany dropped her wine glass and fell to the floor in convulsions.

Leah pointed and let out a high-pitched cry, and then the room grew silent.

Brittany's body jerked once more and fell eerily still.

Chapter Four

AN ODD, hollow feeling filled my brain, and for a half second, I stared, trying to process what I'd seen. What had just happened to Brittany?

Suddenly, as if everyone in the room had also needed time to make sense of what we'd seen, people began to respond.

"Get an ambulance." Cordell yelled. He rushed to Brittany's side, knelt, and took her hand. "Somebody, call 9-1-1!"

"I'm dialing," Nick shouted. His face looked grim, as if he feared the same thing I did, that an ambulance wasn't going to help Brittany. She was far too still.

Mortimer, who had perhaps had emergency training in his work at Grove University, moved toward the hall. "I'll watch for the ambulance and help them find the right room."

"Thank you," I called after him.

"Paula"—Cordell scanned the room until he found her, then gestured to Brittany—"can you help her?"

Paula was already halfway across the room. She knelt by Brittany, opposite Cordell. No longer the first wife making catty comments, she was every bit the calm healthcare professional as she rested two fingers on Brittany's neck.

The rest of us gathered round, watching Paula, and staring at Brittany, whose face looked pinker than normal. Cordell took one of Brittany's smooth, slender hands and held it between his gnarled, age-spotted hands.

Paula's jaw tensed, and she moved her hand slightly on Brittany's neck, then pressed her lips together. "Cordell, I'm not getting a pulse." She began doing chest compressions.

Cordell let out a strangled wail.

Heather gasped, and I heard a faint cry that sounded like Alice.

I glanced across the room at her. Stalwart Alice was pale.

I scanned the room, searching for my staff members.

Imani's eyes were wide, and Rodney had sunk into a chair and was rubbing a hand over his ruddy face.

My mind swirled. How could Brittany be gone? Why did she die the way she did? It didn't seem ... natural.

And why wasn't Paula doing mouth-to-mouth? Was that because she, too, thought Brittany's collapse seemed suspicious?

Even if I didn't understand what had happened, I had to deal with it.

I stood up taller. "Everyone, we need to step back, sit

down, and wait for the emergency personnel to arrive. We, uh, don't want to be in their way."

And we probably shouldn't leave what might be the scene of a crime. But I didn't say that part out loud.

Their faces glazed in disbelief, everyone moved toward the nearest chair.

Another ugly thought came to mind. "As an added precaution, because we don't know what happened to Brittany, I don't think we should eat or drink anything." I glanced at Paula. Was I being paranoid?

"Libby's right," Paula said quickly.

"Oh-hh." Leah, who had not yet sat down, swayed ever so slightly.

My heart rate sped, and I hurried to her side. One guest collapsing was horrible. But two? What if that was only the beginning? "Are you okay?" I asked Leah.

"Just feeling a little faint, I think." She clutched a nearby table, and I helped her to a chair.

"Head between your knees, Mom." Brad rushed over and gently pushed Leah's shoulders forward. "She doesn't do well with blood or ... other medical stuff," he said to the room. His eyes were tense, though, as if he feared it might be something worse.

The next few minutes were a blur. Brad helped Leah lie on the floor and, after a moment, told us he thought she was okay.

Then the paramedics arrived, followed not long after by two members of the Dogwood Springs Police, Officers Tate and Davis, both of whom I'd met before.

One of the paramedics took over for Paula. The other checked on Leah and told us her vitals looked good.

Once I knew Leah was all right, I sat down, feeling like I'd be hypocritical not to, since I'd asked the others to sit. But my view of what the paramedics were doing was partially blocked, and I couldn't hear what they were saying because everyone else had started talking quietly.

Which left me nothing to do but shift back and forth in my seat, trying to see better, and worry. The evening I had worked so hard to plan was a disaster. A complete and utter disaster.

A few minutes later, Detective John Harper entered the room. He and I had met on several occasions over the past year, most related to crimes. He was in his mid-fifties and had a salt-and-pepper buzz cut and thick, dark eyebrows. He shot me a questioning look and talked with one of his officers.

The rest of us watched silently as the paramedics tended to Leah and continued to work on Brittany. Soon, Leah was sitting up, apparently fine. But eventually, the paramedics covered Brittany's body with a sheet.

"My princess," Cordell cried. He covered his face with his hands and sobbed.

Paula, who sat beside him, patted his shoulder and spoke quietly to him.

"Ladies and gentlemen, if you are feeling any ill effects, or if you touched this woman"—Detective Harper gestured to Brittany's body—"after she collapsed, I want the paramedics to make sure you're all right. After that, I'm afraid

I'll need to speak with each of you individually about what happened." The detective moved to block the door to the hall. "While you wait, please remain silent and do not eat or drink anything. Officer Davis will be here in the room with you."

My stomach clenched. I was right. Brittany's death hadn't been natural. I'd seen this police procedure before, at least the part about getting individual statements. It meant a crime had been committed.

Detective Harper turned toward me. "Libby, may I use your office?"

"Yes, yes, of course." I got up, grabbed my purse from where I'd stashed it behind the curtains, and dug out my keys. "Let me unlock it."

The detective, Officer Tate, and I walked down the hall toward my office. I unlocked the door, switched on the light, and reached across the front of my desk to shove my papers to one side.

"Thank you." Detective Harper went around the desk and sat down.

Detective Tate moved one of my two guest chairs to the corner of the room, pulled a notebook from his pocket, and placed it on the chair. "Shall I take Miss Ballard back to the other room, sir?"

The detective nodded. "Yes. Then bring Rodney in first. I assume he knows all the players since his sister is related to these people." He turned to me. "Libby, I'm going to interview you last. Officer Davis is in the room and will give me his impressions later, but you're observant, and I'd appreciate it if you would keep your eyes open, see if you notice anything odd."

"I'd be happy to, but first can I ask you how you think she—"

Before I could ask if Brittany's death seemed natural, the detective angled his head toward the door, and Officer Tate escorted me back to the reception room with the others.

Despite the ego boost at the thought that Detective Harper valued my opinion, the rest of the night dragged on in slow misery. I sat, nervously running a hand over my pearls, exchanging uncomfortable glances with my board members, the mayor, and the three city council members.

No matter how much I wanted to talk with Cordell or any of his family to express my sympathy, the police had requested that we remain silent.

So I did as Detective Harper had requested and watched Cordell and his family.

None of them did anything that seemed particularly odd, but they all looked unhappy.

Cordell sat motionless, like a deflated balloon. The zest for life had escaped, leaving him hunched over, looking ten years older, his face etched with new lines of pain.

At one point, I caught his eye, pressed both hands over my heart, and sent him a sympathetic look.

He nodded and blinked back tears.

The rest of his family didn't appear particularly sad, but they certainly weren't delighted to be there. Paula stayed near Cordell, keeping quiet as the police had requested, but often resting a hand on his arm or gently rubbing his back, as if you might to calm a child. She had a tightness around her eyes that made me think she had a headache, and, like Cordell, she looked older than when she entered the room.

Their daughter, Heather, slumped in a chair at the same table, her mouth half-open as if she was still in shock. Heather's son Emmett sat, not at a table, but in a chair against the wall near the door to the hall.

Leah sat at another table with her two sons. Although she seemed to have recovered, she still appeared a bit pale.

Of all the family members, now that he knew his mom was okay, Leah's son Brad seemed the least bothered by the situation. His face was suitably solemn, but he rocked back in his chair the way my mother always told my brother not to do. Once, he got up and used an andiron to adjust a log in the fireplace.

His brother, Nick, must have inherited more of his mother's tendency toward nervousness. Or perhaps, as an artist, his temperament was more disturbed by seeing Brittany die. He sat facing downward, shoulders drooping, folding and refolding a napkin on the table in front of him.

As for me, I hate to admit it, but once the shock of Brittany's death wore off, my thoughts turned to how her death would affect the museum. Would it be closed for several days, as it had when another tragedy occurred at the museum last summer? Would attendance plummet when people learned someone had died here? And would Cordell even consider donating to the museum or any other organization in town after this tragedy?

Eventually, it was my turn to talk with the detective. While Officer Tate searched my purse, I told Detective Harper what I knew.

I explained that Paula's branch of the family didn't like Leah's branch and vice versa. And that, except for Cordell, all the family members seemed to dislike Brittany.

But Rodney had already told the detective as much, and despite what seemed like good questions from Detective Harper, I didn't have anything else that was useful to impart.

Finally, when the detective paused, I asked my own question. "Was it poison that—?"

"No," he said, cutting me off.

"Really? Because from what I saw, it sure seemed like it might be, and—"

"I mean no, do not go there," he said firmly. "I know you're too nosy for your own good, and I know you've had success solving crimes in the past, Libby. But do not start trying to solve this murder. Because that's definitely what it is. Murder."

"You're sure?"

"I'm sure. We'll have to wait for a full toxicology report, but the scent of almonds was pretty strong. I'm almost certain that woman was poisoned with cyanide."

Chapter Five

EARLIER IN THE WEEK, I envisioned that I'd spend Tuesday morning kicking back in the museum conference room with Rodney and Imani, reveling in the receipt of a large check from Cordell.

Instead, someone had been murdered at the museum, my hopes of receiving that large check were slim, and the building was closed until the police finished collecting evidence.

For now, Alice had urged the board to give Rodney, Imani, and me paid time off until the museum could reopen. The police didn't want us to go into our offices to collect work to do at home and, as Alice quickly convinced the board, we all needed time to recover from the shock of watching Brittany die.

So I sat at my kitchen table midmorning, ignoring the leash that Bella held in her mouth, staring aimlessly out the window at another damp, gray, February day.

What would happen once the museum was allowed to reopen? Would Cordell still donate the money he'd promised?

I couldn't really blame him if he changed his mind. After all, who wants to contribute to the organization that hosted the event where your wife died?

I hated to be thinking only of myself, but the museum needed that elevator. There had been a time around Christmas when Sam hinted that he could donate the funds for an elevator. I'd told him no. He'd already given the museum a historic painting, and I didn't want to take advantage of our relationship. Had that been a mistake?

I let out a heavy sigh. I had more than the possible loss of a donation to worry about. Who wants to even visit a museum where someone was poisoned? What if traces of poison remained in the building? The situation was such a nightmare.

Bella raised one ear and tipped her head at me, then walked back to the other side of the kitchen. She dropped her leash, and it landed with a *clunk* under the hook on the wall where I usually hung it. She came back to my side and rested her head on my knee.

I laid a hand on her head and rubbed her ears. For a long moment, we stayed there, and waves of her love washed over me. The tightness in my shoulders eased, and as I gazed outside, I noticed not only the gray drizzle, but also the cluster of bright yellow daffodils at the back of the yard and a fat robin tugging a worm out of the grass. Then I looked down at my sweet dog, at the essential goodness that shone out of her eyes. "I'm so glad I have you in my life, Bella. If it wasn't for you, I'd forget to think about the positives in life. And there are positives, even in this difficult time. I've got you, I've got Cleo and my other friends, and I've got Sam."

Bella let her tongue hang out in a happy doggy expression that, even in the worst of times, made my heart lighter.

I took a sip of my tea and cradled the mug. "The museum has gone through difficult times before, and the community supported us. If Cordell decides not to go through with his contribution to the museum, I'll just have to keep working to raise funds for that elevator." I set my mug on the table with a *thunk*. "Let's check the radar and see if there will be a break in the storm soon when we can take that long walk you've been wanting."

At the word *walk*, Bella trotted out of the room and returned with my tennis shoes.

See, it wasn't simply my opinion. She really was the smartest dog in town.

I opened the weather app on my phone, but the radar didn't look very promising. Just in case, I started putting on my shoes. I was tying the laces when my doorbell rang.

I opened the door to the entryway and peered out the window by the front door.

Rodney stood on the step, without a raincoat or an umbrella.

I pulled open the door. "Rodney, come in. You're getting soaked." Once he was inside my apartment, I got a clean towel for him from the bathroom.

He dried his face and head and blotted what water he could from his shirt. "Thanks. It wasn't raining when I left the house earlier."

"I don't have coffee." His favorite. "Would you like some tea? At least it would be warm."

"No, I need to talk with you."

I motioned toward the couch.

As soon as he sat down, Bella came over to say hello.

Rodney patted her head, not really noticing her, and she soon found her favorite toy, a stuffed chicken, and lay down near us.

I took the chair facing Rodney. "What's going on?"

"First thing this morning, Detective Harper brought Paula in for questioning. He says that as a pharmacist she would know all about poison. And one of the council members apparently heard her talking about how much she hated Brittany."

I pursed my lips. "Paula may have been more vocal, but I got the impression everyone hated Brittany."

"Pretty much, but Paula's the chief suspect. The detective got a warrant and is searching her house right now for evidence."

My mouth gaped open. Seriously? "He didn't listen to me at all. I told him Paula was the one person in the room who appeared to have a heart, who had been attentive to Cordell."

Rodney twisted the edge of the towel. "That may have done more harm than good. He thinks Paula killed Brittany because she wants Cordell back."

I hadn't even considered that. "Does she?"

"Not that I know of. She cares about him, yes, but she's said more than once that she'd be miserable in the life he lives these days, swanning about, passing out checks, and going to fancy affairs all the time. She was putting up with it this week, but only because she knew the contributions would help Dogwood Springs."

That fit with what I had seen. Paula didn't strike me as a person who drew attention to herself.

I'd met a lot of donors in my career, enough that I often had a sense about them when I met them. There were those, like Cordell, who wanted a spectacle and public adulation. There were those who viewed having their name on a donor plaque or listed in printed materials as a way to indicate the value they saw in the museum and encourage others to donate. And there was a final group, and I'd have guessed Paula fell into this category, who were happier mailing in a check—sometimes quite hefty—and asking to be listed in donor recognition as anonymous.

"Anyway, Paula's really stressed out." Rodney patted his gray hair again with the towel. "Not only for herself, but because she thinks Detective Harper is wasting valuable time focusing on her. Even though the detective asked the family not to leave town while he investigates, she's afraid vital clues will be missed."

I ran a hand down the arm of my chair. "She has a point."

"She does, but I'm more concerned about her. What if Detective Harper arrests her? She's seventy years old, too old to go to prison." He leaned forward, one hand clutching the knee he'd had surgery on last year. "Would you be willing to try to find the killer, Libby? I mean, since you were there, and since it does involve the museum…"

Try to find the killer. Exactly what Detective Harper told me not to do.

But it was one thing to agree to stay out of an investigation—which I hadn't actually done—when you thought the police were going to arrest the real perpetrator. It was another thing to ignore the situation when someone was wrongly accused.

And, although I liked Detective Harper and believed he tried to do his best for the town, I had noticed that he had a tendency to zero in on one suspect and ignore other possibilities. "I do have a hard time believing Paula is a murderer," I said slowly. "I mean, she's your sister, and she might have been outspoken, but she seems like a good person."

"She is." Rodney's voice cracked. "I don't understand how Detective Harper can't see that."

Normally, Rodney was calm, with the occasional twinkle in his eye and a dry, witty comment. I'd never seen him so emotional.

"I assume the detective is following evidence that points to Paula." I sat up taller. "But that just makes me think he's not looking at the right evidence."

Rodney's face brightened.

I was good with puzzles like crosswords and mysteries. I was even, I'll admit, a bit stubborn about solving them. Plus, I'd always been a big advocate for justice and fairness, a believer that rules were meant to be followed. After the way things had worked out with my divorce, those ideas mattered even more to me. If Detective Harper was following the wrong path, justice would never be reached. Even someone like Brittany deserved justice. I hadn't liked the woman, but she didn't deserve to die.

Plus, the sooner the real killer was behind bars, the sooner the museum could put this ugly event in the past.

One could—with a great stretch—consider that solving this case was part of my job description as museum director, under the category of "other duties as needed."

And I would never tackle a mystery alone. My friends had helped me solve mysteries before. "Okay," I said. "I'll try to help Paula."

Rodney's breath whooshed out. "Thank you."

If only I could assure him that I knew I would find the killer. But all I could do was try. And I knew my friends would try as well. "I'll ask Cleo and Alice and Zeke and Sam to help. We've figured out things the police missed in the past. Maybe we can figure this murder out as well."

"I hope so." Rodney got to his feet. "I sure hope so."

I did too.

But still ... cyanide.

A niggle of unease twisted in my gut. This situation could definitely be dangerous. We'd be tangling with someone who had no qualms about using a deadly poison.

Chapter Six

AT A FEW MINUTES before seven that evening, Bella got up from the rug by the fireplace, trotted to the front window, and barked.

The rain had stopped, and I peeked out the window. In the light of the streetlights, I saw a blue Tesla turn into my driveway.

I unlocked the door from my living room to the entryway just as someone knocked on the outside door.

Quickly, I opened both doors.

Sam stood on the porch, looking like the textbook image of a tall, sexy geek in jeans, a leather jacket, and dark, rectangular frame glasses. As usual, his dark hair was rumpled, as if he'd run his hand through it while thinking about some complex coding problem.

"Hey, gorgeous." His chocolate brown eyes sparkled, and his words held a warm note that sent a zing of delight through me.

Bella wiggled past me and squeezed into the doorway next to Sam.

"And hello to you too, Bella." Sam laughed and held a brown paper grocery bag toward me. "May I give this to you? I picked up two flavors of Minnesota's Pride ice cream for us to snack on tonight, peanut butter banana swirl and chocolate coconut bliss."

"Thanks." I took the bag from him. Count on Sam to bring ice cream, even in winter.

"I thought it might help us tonight as we try to figure out this latest murder." He bent down to give me a quick kiss.

Bella barked, and Sam followed me into my apartment, then knelt to say hello to her and shake her offered paw.

Bella liked almost everyone, but lately it seemed that she had become especially fond of Sam. I would always be her favorite human, but Sam now seemed to come in a close second. Maybe it was because his family had a golden retriever when he was a boy and, because of that, he adored Bella. A mutual love fest was right up her alley.

A knock sounded on the door from the front entryway.

I opened it.

Zeke, Cleo's sixteen-year-old nephew, stood near the foot of the stairs to Cleo's apartment. As usual in the winter, he wore a sweatshirt that advertised a computer game, jeans, and black Converse tennis shoes. His long dark hair was pulled back in a ponytail. He gave me a quick wave and helped Cleo climb down the last few stairs and hobble to my couch.

"I might have overdone it today." She pointed to her left ankle, which was swollen above the compression bandage. "I thought I could go into the salon this afternoon, sit with the receptionist, and keep an eye on things."

Right. I had a hard time picturing Cleo remaining seated for more than five minutes at her salon. "Do you need an ice pack?"

"No, but could I have a straight chair to put my foot on?" She frowned down at the injured ankle.

"Of course." I grabbed a chair from my dining table, as well as a small decorative pillow from the other end of the couch, and helped her get situated.

"I bet this has some healing properties." Sam brought her a bowl with a large scoop of each flavor of ice cream.

"I'm sure it does." Approval rang in her voice. Maybe I was the only one who thought ice cream was reserved for warmer months.

Sam angled his head toward the cartons on the dining table and looked at Zeke. "Want some?"

"You bet." Zeke covered the distance to the table so fast that you'd think he was afraid the ice cream would melt before he got there. Tall and lanky, Zeke could probably eat both cartons in one sitting, but he was a polite kid. He returned to sit by Cleo with a fairly reasonable bowl.

A moment later Alice arrived along with her husband. "I hope you don't mind that I brought Doug." She slid an arm around his waist. "He's been out of town a lot when we solved mysteries before, but he's in town now, and—"

"And I want to help," Doug said with a grin.

I'd met Doug at events at the museum. He was a little older than Alice, ran a large mail-order business that sold gift baskets, and had a fringe of gray hair, a gray mustache, and a white beard.

"We'd love to have your help." I brought in another straight chair, so I'd have seating for six, and glanced over at Doug. "Should I put Bella in my bedroom? You're allergic, right?"

Doug sat in one of the two armchairs, called Bella over, and rubbed her ears. "Not anymore. Well, not bothered by it anymore. I saw a specialist up in Columbia who's got the issue under control."

"How wonderful." Not only for Doug, but also for Bella, who seemed delighted with her new friend. I could see why Alice had married Doug. He had the same easy, friendly vibe as she did.

Soon the six of us were all situated in the living room, each with a bowl of ice cream and either a mug of hot tea or a cup of soda. Bella lay on the floor between Doug and Zeke, happily gnawing a dog biscuit. I lit the fire that I'd laid before they arrived, which added a warm glow to the space. In fact, the room had such a cozy, happy family feeling that I almost hated to bring up the murder.

But we had work to do.

I took one more bite of chocolate coconut bliss, reconsidered my "ice cream is really a summer dessert" idea, and rested my spoon in the bowl. "So, did all of you hear what happened?" I looked at each of them.

Donors, Deception & Death

"Brittany Calhoun dropped dead at the reception. She was poisoned, probably with cyanide," Zeke said.

That pretty much covered it.

"It was definitely cyanide," Cleo said. She turned to Doug. "Sue Ann, the dispatcher at the police department is one of my clients. In the past, she's helped us out with a tip or two." Cleo looked around the group. "Late this afternoon, Sue Ann came in to get her nails done. She told me the police found cyanide in Brittany's wine."

I sat back against the couch. "Maria Wilder has to be freaking out." I remembered her proudly refilling glasses at the reception. "I can't in a million years imagine Wild Woods Winery having poison in their wine. Someone must have tampered with the bottle."

"It wasn't in the bottle," Cleo said. "Only that one glass."

A collective "ooh" ran through the group.

"That means the killer had to be someone at the reception, right?" Doug asked.

"It does," I agreed. "There were eighteen people at the reception. So we have seventeen suspects."

Sam pulled his phone out of his pocket. "I'm making some notes here. Seventeen is a lot of suspects to keep track of."

"Not all of those seventeen are people we need to worry about." Alice tapped her chest. "I was one of them, and so was Libby."

"And we can mark off Imani and Rodney," I said.

Sam's eyes narrowed. "But Rodney is related to this family. Shouldn't we consider him as a possible suspect?"

"No," Alice and I said in unison. The idea was logical, exactly what I'd expect from Sam, but he didn't know Rodney like Alice and I did.

"You're right about the relationship, Sam," I said. "Rodney is the younger brother of Cordell's first wife, but there's no way he's the murderer."

"I've sung with him in the church choir for more than twenty years," Alice said. "I'd consider him as trustworthy as Doug." She reached over and squeezed her husband's arm, and her face shone with the type of trust you dream of in a marriage. "Which brings us down to thirteen people."

"Scratch off Cordell as a suspect," I said. "He was way too upset to have killed Brittany. No one is that good of an actor."

Doug's eyes narrowed. "Are you sure? Anytime I watch detective shows on TV, they always consider the spouse."

I glanced over at Alice. A second later, we both nodded our heads. "I'm sure," I said.

Sam ran a finger down the list on his phone. "That brings us down to twelve suspects."

"I think we can rule out Maria Wilder, Mortimer Townsend, the mayor, and the three city council members who were there," I said. "They all wanted the evening to go well so that Cordell would make his donation, and since Brittany lived in Nashville, none of them would have known her."

"I'll ask around to make sure none of them knew her, but I would assume you're right," Alice said.

"Excellent." With all of her local connections, Alice could find out the information easily.

Zeke scooped up a huge spoonful of ice cream but paused with it halfway to his mouth. "So, unless Alice learns differently, that only leaves six people—all family members—to consider as suspects."

Doug held up a finger. "Hold on." He turned to Alice. "Didn't you tell me the event was catered? That's at least one more person who was there."

"You're right." Cleo said. "People always overlook servers and cleaning staff, but they're there, and they can slip in and out almost unnoticed."

"And the caterers provided the wine glasses," Alice said.

"But would they have known Brittany or had any reason to kill her?" I rubbed the back of my neck. "Other than the fact that she was obnoxious and kept requesting changes to her meal?"

"That's not a reason to kill someone," Sam said. "Caterers have to deal with more of that than you'd think."

"So six family members as suspects." Zeke looked at Cleo. "You said they all hated Brittany, right?"

Cleo turned to me.

"They sure seemed to. Let me tell you who's who in the Calhoun family." I went through the family members, trying to make them easy to keep straight.

First, the blond branch of the family. Paula, Rodney's sister, the first wife and retired pharmacist, who Detective Harper suspected. Her daughter, Heather, the occupational therapist, and Heather's adult son, Emmett.

Then the brunette branch of the family. Leah, the second wife who had been Cordell's secretary, and her two sons, Brad and Nick.

"Not that long a list," I said in conclusion. "All we have to do is figure out which one of these people wanted Brittany dead. And why."

Sam looked up from his phone. "This is going to be harder than the previous mysteries we've solved. We don't know any of these people and, except for Paula, they all live out of town. That will make it harder to learn if they're keeping any secrets."

My heart sank. What he said made sense. In the past, we'd been able to rely heavily on Cleo and Alice. Between the two of them, they knew most of the people in Dogwood Springs. I took another spoonful of ice cream, seeking solace in sugar.

Then I looked around the room, at five intelligent people, and I sat up taller. We weren't without resources. Some of them, like Sam and Zeke, were skilled at finding information online. And my friends weren't going to quit and leave me high and dry. Each of these people—even Doug, who I didn't know as well—was someone I could trust to help me.

As if she thought I had forgotten about her, Bella got up and walked over to me, resting her head on my knee. I patted her back.

I didn't only have my six human friends. I also had Bella. After the experiences I'd had since I moved to Dogwood Springs, I wouldn't be surprised if she helped too.

"It is going to be more difficult," I said. "But that doesn't mean it's impossible. If we work together, I really believe we can figure out who killed Brittany Calhoun."

Everyone murmured in agreement.

My heart filled. Just as I thought, these were friends I could count on. "We need to get started, and I suggest we begin by seeing what more we can learn from Rodney and Paula."

A murmur of agreement rose from my friends.

I sent Rodney a text. He checked with Paula, and we arranged for Alice and me to meet him at Paula's the next morning at nine. As long as Paula didn't get arrested first.

Chapter Seven

RIGHT BEFORE NINE the next morning, I parked on the street in front of Paula's house, ready to begin our investigation.

The rain of the previous day was back. Alice had already arrived, and the two of us shared her giant golf umbrella as we picked our way up the steep driveway, avoiding streams of water flowing down the concrete. At last we reached Paula's one-story house, which was perched on the side of a hill.

The house was probably built in the 1970s and had no grass in the front yard, only low shrubs and hunks of limestone scattered here and there, with pockets of daffodils and crocus tucked in around them.

Alice loved plants and was enchanted with the landscaping. I could see the practicality of it, as mowing that slope would have been nearly impossible, but I also remembered helping my mom weed her flowerbeds when I was growing up. I wasn't sure if I'd enjoy weeding an entire front yard.

Alice rang the doorbell, and we heard delicate chimes play inside the house.

There was a brief delay, and then Paula opened the door. Her hair was in slight disarray, and her cheeks were pink.

"Sorry to keep you waiting. I hate to overwhelm visitors, so I was putting the dogs in my bedroom. Elvis was not cooperating." She stepped back. "Please, come in."

We went in and wiped our wet shoes on the mat as Paula took our coats.

"It's fine if you want to let the dogs out," Alice said. "Libby and I both like them."

"Oh, good. They'll be so much happier. Totally spoiled since I retired. I'll be right back." She motioned toward the living room. "Please, have a seat."

I stood for a moment, taking in the living room. Bookshelves filled with hardbacks and paperbacks took up every inch of available wall space. Eventually, I sat by Alice on the brown couch, which had a tweedy look to it, but was actually a rather sleek fabric, one I'd guess was easy to vacuum dog hair from.

There was a scratching sound, and three tubby pugs galloped into the room. They sniffed our shoes and allowed us to pet them while Paula introduced them as Elvis, Buddy, and Fats, named for Elvis Presley, Buddy Holly, and Fats Domino. "My husband was a big fan of early rock and roll," she explained.

The front door opened, and Rodney let himself in

without knocking. He said hello to Alice and me, and then turned to his sister. "Coffee?"

"I was just about to offer. It's all ready."

Alice and I declined, and Rodney said he'd help himself, so Paula sat in a small armchair facing us.

The pugs hurried over to lie at her feet, arranging themselves as if the positions were determined long ago.

I expected Paula to jump right in and tell us about being questioned by the police. Instead, she looked down at the dogs and twisted her hands together in her lap.

"I understand things have been really difficult lately," Alice said softly. "Can you tell us what happened?"

Paula looked up, and tension eased from her shoulders.

Count on calm, soothing Alice to make people feel more comfortable.

"Of course. Sorry." Paula blinked. "Thank you both so much for coming over. My lawyer says the police don't have enough evidence to arrest me yet, but I'm the top suspect." Her lips thinned into a horizontal line. "I admit that I hated Brittany, but I'd never kill a person."

Rodney returned to the living room, holding a steaming mug. "Just because she was a pharmacist and understands poison, doesn't mean she'd use it."

One of the pugs trotted over by Rodney, waited to be petted, and settled down with its head on his shoe.

Rodney smiled down at the dog and then looked back up at us, his face more somber.

If we were going to figure this out, we needed more information. "Paula, can you tell us more about Brittany, about why you didn't like her?" I refrained from mentioning the impression the woman had made on Imani and me.

Paula's jaw tightened. "The reason is simple. I didn't like how she treated Cordell."

I tipped my head in acknowledgment. I hadn't been impressed with how Brittany acted so bored with Cordell's stories myself. Even if she'd heard them many times before, it was only polite to listen, especially if he was sharing them with people at an event in his honor.

"And she was unbelievably selfish," Paula added. "Let me give you an example. Cordell said he wanted to buy a condo on the beach in Florida where he and Brittany could spend January through March next year. They flew down one week in early February and toured several units. The day of the murder, Cordell arranged for us all to have lunch together at the café downtown, and he started talking about the condo idea." She looked over at me. "You remember that Brad has two young sons?"

"Yes. Cordell mentioned them."

Paula nodded. "So when Cordell was telling us about the condos they'd seen, just as calmly as you please, as if she didn't even realize how rude it was, Brittany told us she was lobbying for a two-bedroom unit instead of a three-bedroom because she didn't want to have enough space for Brad's boys to visit."

I stared at Paula, struggling to wrap my brain around what Brittany had said. Talk about selfishness.

"Goodness," Alice said.

"And she said this in front of both Cordell and Brad," Paula said. "His boys are three and five, too young, of course, for all the events this week, so they're home with their mom. But they're fairly well-behaved, sweet little kids, and Cordell adores them. They're his only grandkids, besides our grandson Emmett, and he's all grown up. The very idea that Brittany would want to reduce the amount of time Cordell got to spend with those little boys..." Paula's eyebrows pinched together. "Is it any wonder someone killed that woman?"

Honestly, I agreed, but even though she'd been quite a piece of work, Brittany didn't deserve to be murdered. "Do you think Brad might have been so offended by her comment that he killed her?"

Paula quickly shook her head. "No. I'm not trying to point the finger at Brad. I talked with him after she made that nasty comment, and he said the less time his kids were around Brittany, the better. He simply planned to invite Cordell to spend time with the kids at his house when all of them were in Nashville."

Alice looked off to one side, eyes narrowed, as if still bothered by Brittany's nasty temperament, then turned back to Paula. "Then is there anyone who you do suspect? Someone who had a good motive?"

Paula barked out a laugh. "That's the hard part. Any member of the family, me included, had an excellent motive. You do know that Brittany was one of Cordell's estate attorneys before they married, don't you?"

I looked over at Alice, who seemed as surprised as me.

"We had no idea. I hadn't even known Brittany was a lawyer."

"She was. She worked for a well-respected firm in Nashville. Got a job there right out of law school, working in estate planning. After she and Cordell got married, she 'retired,' at age twenty-seven. But she was apparently a legal whiz kid, and she was trying to convince Cordell to change his will so that she'd get all his money."

Ooh. No wonder the rest of the family hated her. "How is the will currently written?" I asked.

"The money and shares of Cordell's business are divided evenly. Most of it is split three ways, between Leah, Brittany, and me. There are also very generous—as in seven-figure generous—bequests to each child and grandchild, with the assets for Brad's kids put in a trust until they're older."

"Cordell's sold a lot of fried chicken," Rodney said. "His company's valued at about two hundred fifty million dollars. Certainly enough to provide plenty of motive for killing Brittany and keeping that will the way it is."

"Wow." I tried to wrap my brain around the idea of inheriting millions of dollars. "That is a lot of motive, an awful lot of motive."

For a moment, we all sat silently.

"Tell us a little more about your family," Alice said. "You have the one daughter?"

Paula gestured to the wall near the door that led to the dining room. A large portrait showed Paula with blonder hair, Heather about thirty pounds lighter, a dark-haired man with a devilish grin, and Emmett when he was probably in high school.

"Yes, just the one." She looked down at her hands. "I actually got pregnant in high school. That's why Cordell and I got married, but we lost that baby, our son. A couple years later we had Heather, but we'd gotten married too young. We both had a lot of growing up to do."

"Oh, Paula," Alice said gently. "I'm sorry you lost your first child."

"Thank you." Paula paused. "Anyway, our parents helped us a lot, watching Heather so we both could get our degrees. I sometimes wondered if the two of us might have gotten along better if we'd met when we were older, but as it was, we fought a lot. I wasn't totally shocked that we eventually got divorced."

"But Heather turned out well," Rodney said.

"She did. She's been honored by the clinic system where she works. She and her husband live in Knoxville. Emmett, their son, lives in Durham, North Carolina."

"They're good people, all of them," Rodney said.

Most likely, Rodney's assessment was correct, but I had to keep an open mind. I couldn't rule out three of our suspects on his word alone. Yes, they were his family, but how well did Rodney know them if they lived so far away?

Alice gazed at the portrait another moment, then turned to Paula. "I assume we should talk to Cordell next to ask if he knew of someone who might have wanted to kill Brittany."

Paula gave a wry smile. "I'm afraid it would be a waste

of time. He's in total shock. Part of him—the part that was smart enough to build a fast-food empire—realizes that the killer almost has to be a member of the family. But emotionally, he can't process that. Or the fact that anyone would have wanted to kill Brittany. That girl had him so bewitched he can't imagine anyone not adoring her."

"Well, is there any member of the family that you think might have a stronger motive for killing Brittany?" I asked. "Maybe someone who would be especially hurt if Cordell changed his will?"

Paula shifted in her seat and reached down and rubbed the back of the nearest pug, a slightly less pudgy fellow that I thought was Buddy.

Rodney glanced over at Paula. "Tell them what you told me."

"It's only a theory, and I hate to put someone else in the same position as me, having people wrongly suspect them," she said.

"Sis, it's a good theory. I think Libby and Alice and their friends should check into it, especially since you said the police didn't seem to take you seriously."

She gave a slight shrug. "That's probably why I feel awkward discussing it. Because the cops thought I was trying to shift the blame. But you're right, Rodney."

She turned to face Alice and me. "Leah's youngest son, Nick, is an artist. He makes pottery. Really attractive pieces." She pointed to a purple and green vase about ten inches tall on one of her bookshelves.

It was quite pretty. Different enough to be unique, but

not so different that it stuck out in a room. I could see why Paula liked it, even if it was made by Leah's son. I looked back at Paula, eager to hear more.

"Right before Christmas, Nick asked Cordell to give him money to start a gallery where he could sell his work. Cordell said Nick believes the country music crowd, some of whom have plenty of money to burn, will be a really lucrative market. Since Nick also lives in Nashville, he thought a gallery would be perfect."

"But Cordell said no?" I asked.

"He did. And—now this is just a guess on my part—but I imagine Brittany discouraged Cordell from investing."

"It makes sense," Alice said. "If she wanted all the money to come to her."

"That's what I thought," Paula said. "And Nick might have thought that if Brittany was out of the picture, he'd have more luck convincing Cordell to bankroll a gallery."

I considered the idea. "It does give Nick an immediate need for money, which seems like a stronger motive than concern about the will. After all, there was always a chance, if Cordell changed his will to give all the money to Brittany, that he could always change it back."

"Unless Brittany, being an estate lawyer, had documents drawn up that meant Cordell's decision couldn't be changed. Emmett mentioned that there are ways to set up your estate that can't be revoked." Paula tipped her head to one side. "But still, if I had to pick a family member with the most motive, I'd pick Nick."

"Then that's who we will talk to next," I said. "He's staying at the Hilltop Bed and Breakfast?"

"Everyone in the family is, except me," Paula said. "Even Heather and Emmett. Cordell was paying and, well, as much as I love my daughter and grandson, we're all happier with our own space."

We chatted a few minutes longer, Paula and Rodney both thanked us profusely, and Alice and I left, promising to talk to Nick.

Chapter Eight

ALICE and I carefully made our way down the wet driveway, once again sharing her big golf umbrella to protect us from the rain. We said goodbye, and I climbed in my car, thinking that Detective Harper had to be insane to suspect Paula Calhoun of murder.

He probably wasn't going to change his mind unless my friends and I were able to find a better suspect, and right now that looked like Nick. But how could I initiate a conversation with Nick? I didn't want him to know I suspected him or—

My phone rang.

I dug it out of my purse and answered.

"Libby, this is John Harper. We've finished collecting evidence at the museum."

A zing of excitement shot through me, followed immediately by unease. I liked the idea of going back to work until I thought about walking in the room where Brittany had been poisoned. "What did you find?"

"There were traces of cyanide in the glass Brittany dropped to the floor and in the rug where the wine had spilled, but nowhere else."

Hmmm. 'Nowhere else' sounded good, but my chest still felt tense. "What about the vial or little packet or whatever the killer used to carry in the poison?"

"Most likely that was a glass or metal vial to prevent the poison from being absorbed through the skin." The detective blew out a loud breath. "Unfortunately, despite the fact that officers searched each person before they allowed them to leave, I think the killer managed to sneak the vial out with them when they left."

Uh-oh. That didn't sound good for Officers Tate and Davis. But I had other issues to worry about—the people at the museum. "Is the museum safe for guests? And for people to work there?" If something happened to a guest or Imani or Rodney or one of the volunteers, I'd never forgive myself.

"My team went over the building thoroughly and took samples of all the food and drink, as well as the dust in every room. We found no further evidence of cyanide. We believe the killer was very careful. After all, they wouldn't want to risk poisoning themselves. I think it's safe to open the museum to the public."

The tension in my chest eased. "Thank you." What he said made sense. If someone was dealing with cyanide, they would think about their own safety. And clearly, the police had been in the museum for the past two days without any ill effects.

"We'll need to keep that area rug that was in front of the fireplace for evidence," Detective Harper said.

"I can tell you, as the director, the museum never, ever wants that rug back." I shuddered. What if some trace of poison remained in the fibers and some little kid sat down on the rug and got it on their skin? "We would have to remove it anyway when we remodel the room to use as display space. It's not appropriate for people with mobility issues."

"Very good. I'll have an officer take down the crime scene tape, and the next time a local reporter calls to ask about the murder, I'll be sure to tell them that the museum is safe to visit." He cleared his throat. "Now the only remaining thing to discuss is to make sure you're being safe. You are staying out of this murder investigation, aren't you?"

Well no. In fact, I had a lead that I planned to check into, Paula's theory about Nick, the theory the detective had already rejected. So I couldn't actually say I was staying out of the investigation. "I, uh—"

I heard another person's voice over the phone line, like someone had come into Detective Harper's office.

"I've got to go," he said. "Don't do anything stupid, Libby."

He hung up.

Talk about a timely interruption. I smiled and sent a text to the staff and the museum board to let them know that tomorrow we could resume normal operations at the museum, and I asked Imani to email the volunteers.

Then I started the car and turned toward downtown. The museum still had issues—big issues—but reopening was a step forward. It was time to visit the Dogwood Café for a celebratory muffin.

The museum could open, and if Detective Harper asked, I could honestly say that I hadn't done anything stupid. At least not so far. All I'd done was talk with Rodney, his sister, and Alice, and think about talking to Nick. Although I was sure the detective would say I was being nosy, I knew the truth. This wasn't about my curiosity. This was about justice.

~

By the time I found a parking spot downtown, the rain had changed to a fine mist. I left my umbrella in the car and walked to the café.

The place was about half-full, scattered with tourists, retirees, and even a few businesspeople who were conducting meetings at the highly polished wooden tables. Who could blame them for preferring the café to their offices? It was such a snug space, with soft conversation, the occasional clink of silverware against plates, and rich caramel-brown walls that made a cold day feel warmer.

I made my way to a small table in the back and took a seat.

"What can I get you?" The server pulled a notepad from her apron.

"I'll have a cranberry orange muffin and a large hot tea, English Breakfast if you have it." The tea at the café wasn't as good as the Yorkshire tea I kept at home, but it was better than average, and the café's muffins were fabulous.

"Coming right up." The server slipped away.

I sat back in my chair and breathed in the rich aroma of bacon and coffee that filled the air. Even though I didn't like to drink coffee or have it in a dessert, I loved the smell of it. As for bacon, well, who didn't like the smell of bacon?

I was reconsidering my order, wondering if I should have chosen a breakfast sandwich made with bacon when, out of the corner of my eye, I saw someone enter the café.

I jerked my head around. Yes! It was Nick. The very person I wanted to talk to, walking right into my path.

I sat up taller and waved, hoping I could convince him to join me.

He didn't even look in my direction. Instead, he took the first table near the door—one where I could have told him he'd get a blast of cold air every time someone came in—and started talking to a server.

Drat. How was I going to do this?

I'd have to join him at his table.

As smoothly as I could, so as not to attract his attention, I stood, scooped up my coat and purse, and hurried to the counter where my server was fixing my tea.

"I'm sorry," I whispered to her. "But I need my order to go."

The guy beside her turned on some complex-looking coffee machine that whirred like it was about to lift off.

"To go?" my server said at top volume.

"Yes, to go," I whispered. I pressed a finger against my lips. "I'll just stand here and wait for it."

She raised one eyebrow but gave me a thumbs-up and moved my muffin from a plate to a brown paper bag. She slid a cardboard sleeve around a paper cup and decanted my tea into the cup.

I dug in my wallet and pulled out eight dollars, more than enough for the food and a tip. "Keep the change," I said.

I glanced over at Nick, who was gazing out the window. Hopefully, he hadn't seen me. At least he wasn't staring at me, wondering what I was up to.

As nonchalantly as possible, I strolled toward the door, then stopped near his table as if I'd just noticed him. "Oh, hello." I sat my to-go cup and food on the table and stuck out a hand. "You're Nick Calhoun, right? I'm Libby Ballard, from the museum. Remember?" I gave him my friendliest smile.

At first, he didn't look nearly as thrilled to see me. Good manners won out, though, and he quickly rose and gestured to the other chair.

Victory!

"I can only stay a moment," I said. "But I wanted to express my sympathy for your family's loss. What happened the other night was ... so horrible."

His face tensed as if he was in real pain. "Thank you,"

he said quietly. For a member of a branch of the family that hated Brittany, it was an impressive job of acting like he was sorry she died. But maybe he was a nice person and didn't think that simply because he didn't like a woman, she should die.

A server brought him a coffee and a paper bag. "Here's the sandwich you ordered for later," she said.

He thanked her and took a long sip of his coffee.

I intentionally narrowed my eyes, as if I was trying to remember something. "You're the artist, right? The one who makes that lovely pottery?"

"I am." His face brightened. "You've seen my work?"

"Only one piece," I said. "A vase that Paula owns, but it's really gorgeous."

His chest swelled. "Thank you."

Maybe it was the praise, or maybe the hit of caffeine, but his shoulders relaxed. "You know, my dad told me I was crazy, becoming an artist. 'You'll never make a living,'" he said, making his voice lower so he sounded almost exactly like Cordell.

"Making a living as a creative can be difficult," I admitted.

"All I needed was some startup money," Nick said with a note of bitterness. "Dad wouldn't give me a penny, but a couple months ago, I found a patron who helped me set up a gallery. Between sales there and business online, I should be able to make a decent profit by this time next year."

"Wow." I sat back. "That's impressive." I had a friend back in Philly who was a painter, and she and her husband depended heavily on his income as an architect. "You must be a good businessman as well as a talented artist."

He gave a nonchalant shrug.

If Nick had a patron who helped him start his gallery, it blew a hole in Paula's theory. Even if Brittany had convinced Cordell not to fund the gallery, which had only been speculation on Paula's part, Nick had found other funding. His motive for killing Brittany wasn't any stronger than any of the other members of the family. Plus, I remembered him coming over during the reception to talk with Cordell and Brittany. Unlike most of the family, he hadn't acted like he hated her.

I couldn't know for sure, but it seemed rather unlikely that Nick was the killer.

He angled his head to one side. "Is the museum open?"

"We reopen tomorrow," I said.

"Do you think it would be weird if I came in to see that Clayton Smithton painting you have?"

A ripple of pride ran through me. The painting, which Sam had found in his attic and donated to the museum, was a real draw. "I don't think it would be weird at all. The painting is on the first floor, nowhere near where Brittany died." I took a drink of my tea. "And the police say the building is safe."

"Okay, I'll come by," he said. "The cops won't allow us to leave town, and I'd really like to see it."

"Wonderful." I loved it when people from out of town realized all that our little museum had to offer. "I hope the police solve this soon. I'm sure you'd like to get on with your life, and the criminal needs to be brought to justice."

He nodded and leaned toward me. "I got a text from my mom telling me that Brittany was poisoned with cyanide. Personally, I wouldn't even know where to buy cyanide. If you ask me, I think the police need to focus on people who know about drugs and science and stuff." He sat for a moment, as if pondering what he'd said, then stood. "It's been nice talking with you, but I've got to be going."

"It's been nice talking with you as well," I said. "I hope to see you at the museum."

He slipped on his coat and left.

I sent a group text to my friends, filling them in on what Alice and I had learned so far.

Then I unwrapped my muffin and sat there, eating it and thinking about what Nick had said.

Paula, of course, was the suspect who knew about drugs, which was why the police suspected her.

But was there anyone else on our list who would have the technical knowledge to feel comfortable handling cyanide?

Chapter Nine

WHEN I LEFT THE CAFÉ, the rain had stopped, and the temperature had warmed up. It was still chilly but probably above forty. Bella and I could take the walk that we'd skipped earlier in the morning.

The drive home only took a couple of minutes, but it was long enough for me to get antsy. The more I thought about it, the more I realized that if Detective Harper arrested Paula, he'd probably let the rest of the family leave town. My friends and I needed to work fast if we were going to figure out who killed Brittany.

As soon as I got home, before I even got out of the car, I sent another group text to my friends, asking them to meet me at the café for lunch if they could.

Yes, I would be going right back to the café an hour after I left, and, yes, Dogwood Springs did have other delicious restaurants. But the smell of bacon still lingered at the edge of my memory. One of the café's BLTs would be perfect for lunch.

To my surprise, everyone replied to say they would meet me at noon. Cleo's ankle was much better, so she was seeing clients again, but she'd had a cancellation and thought sitting down to eat was a good idea. Alice said both she and Doug were coming and that he planned to buy lunch for us all. Sam had a break between classes. And Zeke said the school superintendent had been fooled by the weather forecast. He thought the town would get ice and called a snow day, but the ice went north of Dogwood Springs and all we got was rain. Zeke was so gleeful about his day off that his text included three exclamation points. He even offered to be Cleo's chauffeur, picking her up and dropping her back at the salon.

Bella and I took our regular route on our walk, down Elm Street to Thirteenth and back, avoiding puddles as much as we could. For once, Bella didn't see any squirrels, the furry creatures that were her own personal nemesis, so there was little barking. A couple of blocks from home, she found a stick, which she proudly carried all the way to our back door, where I convinced her to store it near the doormat. Once we were inside, I dried her feet and filled her food and water bowls, then apologized for the fact that the café didn't allow dogs inside. I rubbed her ears, told her how much I loved her, and headed out.

When I arrived back at the café, Sam had claimed our favorite inside table, the one in the corner farthest from the door, and soon we were all situated. I sat in the middle on one side of the table, with Sam on one side of me and Alice on the other. Cleo sat across from me, Zeke across from Sam, and Doug across from Alice. I settled happily into my chair. There was something comforting about eating with friends, being a regular in a restaurant, and having a spot that felt like it was yours.

A server came to our table almost immediately to take our food and drink orders, and I ordered the BLT I'd been dreaming of, along with coleslaw and hot tea.

I waited until he left, then spoke. "I'm really worried that our suspects will leave town before we solve this. We need to start gathering information faster."

"I have some info already," Sam said. "After you texted that Nick found a patron a couple of months ago, I did some digging online, and I found evidence to support what he said. It was right about that time that he began investing in his business, opening a storefront for his gallery and hiring a salesperson to work there."

"That's great information," I said. "It confirms that Nick basically had the same motive as everyone else in the family for killing Brittany, because she was trying to get Cordell to change his will, but not a stronger motive related to his gallery."

"I checked into Mortimer, Maria, the mayor, and the three city council members," Alice said. "I don't think any of them knew Brittany, so we were right in our initial assessment of six suspects."

"Thanks, Alice." Our assumption had made sense, but I was glad to have it verified.

"This morning, I texted Sue Ann, the police dispatcher, to confirm her next hair appointment," Cleo said. "I asked if there was any news."

"And?" Doug looked at Cleo eagerly.

"The police didn't find anything on Brittany's computer or phone that would explain why someone would kill her." Cleo sighed. "But Sue Ann did say that if she learned anything, she'd let me know."

"So not a clue, but a good step," I said. "It may help us in the long run."

The server brought our drinks. As soon as he left, we resumed our conversation.

"I went through Brittany's social media." Zeke slid the wrapper off his straw and wadded it into a ball. "I was surprised how much she made public. It's almost like she thought she was some kind of minor celebrity. Anyway, I've never seen so many pictures of manicures and posts about clothes. She was more self-absorbed than the popular girls at the high school. About the only thing I found is that Brittany seemed less whiny after Christmas, but that may be because Cordell bought her a new Mercedes."

"Now that's a relationship built on a solid foundation." Doug's eyes twinkled.

The rest of us laughed.

"Do we know anything else?" I looked around the table.

"I don't think so," Alice said.

The others agreed.

"Well, then, speaking of relationships but changing the subject a bit"—Sam turned to Cleo—"how did your date go with my friend last week? He's been out of town at a conference, and I haven't had a chance to ask him."

Cleo ran a hand through her hair, which, as always, fell perfectly back into place. "He's a really nice guy, Sam, and I appreciate you setting us up, but..."

Sam waved her comment aside. "No worries."

Cleo bit her lower lip. "We just didn't have a lot in common, and, well, actually, I heard something about Bryce at the shop the other day."

Alice and I, who both knew the Cleo-Bryce backstory, exchanged glances.

Almost five years ago, Cleo had moved back from New York to Dogwood Springs, hoping to get back together with her high school boyfriend, Bryce Parker, a local vet. Before Cleo moved, she heard that Bryce had broken up with his girlfriend, but by the time Cleo relocated, the couple had made up and gotten engaged.

"What did you hear about Bryce?" Alice asked Cleo.

"Apparently, he and Darcy are having real problems. Darcy's been pushing him to finally set a wedding date and word is that he's getting cold feet."

I tried my best not to look incredulous. I mean, sure, there was a chance that Bryce and Darcy would call off their engagement and he'd fall madly in love with Cleo again, but to me, it seemed more likely, since Bryce and Darcy had been engaged for so many years, that they'd eventually work things out. Or that he wouldn't want to date anyone after being in a relationship for so long.

From the way Cleo's mouth tightened, I had to guess I

didn't do a very good job of hiding my thoughts. She suddenly sat up taller, with a wide smile that didn't quite reach her eyes. "What's new at the high school, Zeke?"

Zeke blinked and dropped the straw wrapper he'd been playing with. "School is as boring as ever, but I do have news." Zeke looked straight across the table at Sam. "You know how my dad only wanted me to apply to his alma mater for college so that I could pledge his fraternity?"

"It's not a bad school," Sam said, but his tone implied Zeke could do better.

Zeke's chest swelled. "Dad might be okay with me going someplace else, as long as I can get scholarship money. I think he was afraid I'd want to go to Harvard or something and expect him to pay for it all. Anyway, he's on board with me applying other places."

"Excellent." Sam reached across the table to give Zeke a fist bump. "Let's talk soon about where you should apply. I think you can definitely get some significant scholarships."

Zeke's eyes lit. "Sweet. Thanks, Sam."

"You've been such a big help to Zeke," Cleo said to Sam. "It was so nice of you to suggest he take the one class at the university while he's still in high school and to get him that part-time job in a computer science lab on campus."

Zeke nodded. "Once I told Dad I'd pay the application fees with money I earned myself, his whole attitude changed."

I glanced over at Sam, and a warm tingle curled around my heart.

Doug elbowed Alice. "Aren't you going to tell them your news?"

Embarrassment flashed through her eyes. "I wasn't going to..."

Alice had news?

She cleared her throat. "I, um, I went to Grove University the other day and talked to them about taking classes as an older student. Even though it's been decades since I graduated high school, the woman there was really nice and said she'd help me figure out one class to take over the summer. In the fall, I'll be able to take more. She even said I might get a few credit hours for 'life experience.'"

Doug wrapped an arm around her shoulders and squeezed. "I'm so proud of her. I'd already graduated college when we met, and I always wished she could get her degree when we were younger."

"I wanted to, but once we had kids, it didn't seem possible," Alice said. "They're all grown though, so the only thing that's been holding me back lately has been ... well, me."

The rest of us congratulated her, and Sam offered to give her a tour of campus and show her some quiet spots for studying and where to get the best coffee.

"Thanks." Alice may not have wanted to share her news, but she sat taller now that she had.

Zeke pointed toward the kitchen. "Hey, I see our food coming this way. What if, while we eat, we each take a suspect and look through their social media? We might find something."

"Zeke, that's brilliant." I beamed at him. "I only know what Rodney told me. I don't think he knows much about Leah and her kids, and he might not have interpreted something about Heather or Emmett the same way we would."

"But surely all our suspects aren't as egotistical as Brittany," Cleo said. "Won't they limit who can see their social media posts?"

"You never know," Sam said. "There are lots of reasons someone might set their social media posts to be public. An artist like Nick might use it to connect to his audience. People who don't spend a lot of time on social media might not have realized you can change the setting. Or some people are so outgoing that they genuinely want to meet new people online."

Zeke leaned back to let the server set down his plate. "Then there are those who know that anything you post on social media can be screenshot and shared anyway, so they don't care if their posts are public. They think of anything they put online as in the public view."

"Wow. So we might find more than I'd expect," Cleo said.

We divided up our suspects, and for the next fifteen minutes, the six of us did exactly as Zeke suggested. Doug looked into Brad, Sam checked on Nick, Alice took Paula, Cleo picked Heather, and I took Leah.

I dove into my BLT, which was even yummier than I'd imagined with crispy bacon, crunchy iceberg lettuce, and tomatoes that were deep red and rich with flavor despite the fact that it was February. By the time I finished, I'd read months of social media posts. I looked around the table. "Let's discuss what we learned. I can report that Leah still lives in Nashville, in the house she and Cordell once shared."

Cleo's forehead wrinkled. "How did you learn that?"

"She shared pictures of a room she said used to be her ex-husband's home office that she turned into a home gym." I held up my phone to show everyone. "But she doesn't work and doesn't appear to volunteer or serve on any community boards. Mostly, it seems she travels, spends money, and exercises." I'd read dozens and dozens of posts about classes at the gym and new workout clothes. "I assume she got a hefty divorce settlement from Cordell."

Hopefully, someone else learned something more useful.

Doug pushed back his plate and gestured with his phone. "Brad Calhoun has his social media pretty locked down, but I was able to learn some about him from his business site. He runs a jewelry manufacturing business. His wife is the designer. I don't know much about jewelry, but their products are at a good price point. Like his mom, he lives in Nashville."

"Nothing suspicious?" Zeke asked.

"Not from the little I could see," Doug said.

"Bummer." Zeke took a drink of his cherry Coke.

Sam laid his phone on the table. "As I suspected, Nick uses social media to promote his pottery, but I didn't learn a lot more about him than what I saw earlier. He also lives in Nashville. He's gotten some regional awards for his pottery, but nothing that seemed like a really big deal. Oh, and he likes to water ski and—probably like most people in Nashville—listens to country music." Sam took a sip of his coffee. "I didn't find a single thing, though, that makes him seem particularly guilty. Who's next?"

Alice waved a hand. "I'll go. Even though Paula is Rodney's sister, and I've known her casually for years, I tried to be unbiased. I'm friends with her online, so I read all her posts. I also texted a friend of mine who knows her better." Alice glanced down at a small notepad beside her phone. "Paula has lived in Dogwood Springs all her life, except for a short time when she was married to Cordell, and they lived in St. Louis. She worked as a pharmacist at the Dogwood Springs Hospital for most of her career."

Oh, yeah. I remembered Rodney telling Imani and me that.

"I'm in every gardening group in town," Alice continued. "So I know Paula's not a member of any of them, but from the pictures she shares online, she seems like quite an accomplished gardener."

A gardener, huh?

Alice held up a hand to stop me. "Before you begin telling me about some murder mystery you read, I have to tell you that fifty years ago, a gardener might have had cyanide on hand to use as a pesticide, but not today. Honestly, I find it hard to picture someone like Paula, who worked in healthcare, as a murderer. I think there has to be a better suspect."

"Well, I don't think it's Heather," Cleo said. "She and her

husband live in Knoxville, and she seems really nice, appears to love her occupational therapy patients, and spends her free time doing crafts." Cleo jiggled her straw in the ice in her glass. "I can tell you from experience, since I have frequent-buyer miles at the craft store, they don't sell cyanide. And Heather's husband seems like a decent guy. He runs a garage that specializes in repairing expensive foreign cars."

I blew out a frustrated breath. "That means, based on who would know how to use cyanide, that the most likely suspect we have at this point is the same one as the police—Paula." Sam had been right, earlier, when he said this investigation would be hard, with almost all our suspects from out of town.

"Not so fast." Zeke held up his phone. "Listen to what I learned about Emmett. Like we knew before, he lives in Durham, North Carolina. He's into bourbon taste testing, is a big fan of an indie band that, personally, I think is really lame, and he thinks duck hunting is the coolest thing ever. The big news is that he's a research chemist." Zeke sat back as if waiting for us to applaud.

"Zeke, that's excellent," I said. "If I had to think of a career where you'd understand how to poison someone with cyanide without endangering yourself, research chemist is near the top of the list."

The others murmured in agreement.

Now that we had a suspect, I wasn't wasting any time. "Let me see if Emmett's at the B & B. I could drive right over and just happen to bump into him." I scrolled through the contacts on my phone and dialed the owner, Faye Burke, who had been a friend of my mom's since she was in high school.

"You shouldn't go alone," Alice said.

Hmmm. Ordinarily, I'd ask Cleo to join me. She'd taken self-defense classes when she lived in New York, and was naturally chatty, which sometimes made suspects talk. With her ankle still healing, though, I was hesitant to ask.

Surely one of my other friends would have time for a little more sleuthing. If not, Faye could probably make a point to be with me if I asked.

A couple of minutes later I hung up. "Drat. According to Faye, Emmett and Heather left half an hour ago. They didn't say where they were headed, but Heather mentioned that they wouldn't be back until late tonight."

"Tomorrow, then?" Alice said. "I could go with you over lunch."

I looked over at Doug. How did he feel about Alice questioning a suspect?

Apparently, fine. He was nodding.

"Perfect." I grinned at Alice. "Tomorrow we'll see what we can learn from Emmett."

Chapter Ten

"CAN I SEE NOW?" I twisted in a chair at Cleo's kitchen table that evening, glancing toward her bathroom where I could check my hair in the mirror.

"One more minute," Cleo said. "Close your eyes."

I squeezed them shut, and a mist of hairspray descended.

"Now you can look." She limped to a nearby chair, winced, and sat down.

"Oh, I knew you shouldn't have done my hair and makeup after a long day at the salon. Your ankle hurts." I'd tried to convince her I could get ready by myself, but she'd rolled her eyes and muttered something about not wanting me to look like I was going to prom in 2009.

She waved me toward the bathroom. "I'll ice my ankle after you leave. What good is it having a best friend who owns their own salon if they don't fix your hair and makeup for a big event like the awards ceremony tonight at Grove University?"

I hurried to the bathroom and looked in the mirror.

My breath caught. Was that really me? I picked up a hand mirror and checked what Cleo had done from the back and the sides. A tingle of amazement grew in my chest.

My hair was pulled up in what I'd call a loose chignon, with tendrils curled around the sides. It was casual, sophisticated and, I had to admit, a thousand times classier than anything I could have created. She'd used more makeup than I normally did, but it wasn't overdone. My skin looked a whole lot better than it ever did with a quick smear of drugstore-brand foundation, my lips were a pale, understated pink, and all the focus was drawn to my green eyes, which she'd made dark and smoky.

"Holy cow! I look, well, I look—"

"You look fabulous," Cleo said. "Change from your robe into that dress, and I'll get a photo before you go downstairs."

I went into her bedroom, where I'd laid my new emerald green dress on the bed. I quickly changed, put on black heels, my pearls, and pearl drop earrings. Then I admired the complete effect in Cleo's full-length mirror. The hair, the makeup, the high slit on the leg, and the V-neck that showed just enough cleavage. Frankly, I was still a little stunned as I went back in the kitchen.

Cleo let out a long, low whistle. "Very nice. Very nice

indeed. Stand over near those plants in the window for the picture. We don't need the fridge in the background."

I posed as requested, then gave her a big hug, careful not to mess up all her work. "I don't know how to thank you. It's way better than I ever could have done."

"My pleasure," she said. "Now, hurry downstairs. Sam should be here any minute."

I thanked her again, got her situated on the couch with an ice pack, and carefully navigated the slightly wonky stairs of our historic house in my heels. I barely had time to give Bella an extra bit of love and a dog biscuit before there was a knock at the door.

I drew in a deep breath, went to the entryway, and opened the outside door.

Sam stood on the porch in a tuxedo. His dark hair was neatly combed. The whisper of a beard that he sometimes wore had been shaved away. And his eyes grew wide in a way that made me warm all over.

"Man," he said. "That is some dress. You look incredible."

"Thanks." I motioned him in and caught a hint of his cologne. Then I gazed at him for a moment, taking in his broad shoulders, perfectly tailored tux, and chiseled jaw. "You look pretty incredible yourself."

It was hard to believe I was going out with this man—this deliciously handsome, brilliant, incredibly rich man. For a woman like me, who a year ago had been newly divorced and unemployed, this was a definite "pinch-me-and-prove-it's-real moment."

But I couldn't stand there gawking all night. I didn't want to make Sam late for an event where he would be honored. "Let me get my purse." I stepped into my bedroom.

Instead of my enormous tote, I'd wedged my phone and a few items into an evening bag the size of a paperback novel. Seriously, how did women manage with small purses? I had to leave all sorts of things I considered essentials behind. Just one more way we women suffered for beauty.

As I came back into the living room, Bella trotted over, wagged her tail, and rubbed her head against Sam's leg, leaving golden hair all over his black pants.

"I'm so sorry," I said.

"Don't be." He gave his pants a half-hearted brush with his hands. "I'll take Bella's love and approval any day over the opinion of someone who might disapprove of a little dog hair." He scratched Bella's ears, told her she was the best dog in the whole state of Missouri, and took my arm. "Shall we?"

I nodded. Ready or not, it was time to make my first appearance with Sam at Grove University.

~

The faculty awards banquet was being held in the newest building at Grove University, the domed, three-story redbrick Felderman Hall, named in honor of an alum who'd made a sizeable donation to the school. On this late

February evening, lights from the dome shone out, announcing to all of campus that something important was taking place.

"I can't park close enough for you to walk in those shoes," Sam said as he pulled up in front of a well-lit door, flanked by potted evergreens. "Let me drop you off here. Please, find your name tag from the table and go on into the event. I'll be with you as soon as I've parked." He got out and opened my door. "There should be a seating chart, and my boss's wife, Dallas McAllister, said she'd watch for you. You can't miss her, she's a tall, Black woman who laughs a lot. Really loudly."

He wanted me to go in alone and hang out with his boss's wife? I was tempted to ask how far I'd have to walk if we went in together. A warm front had passed through, so it wasn't that chilly this evening. But my better judgment—and an ugly memory of the time I walked six blocks in these heels back in Philly—won out. I scooped up my little purse and took Sam's hand as he helped me out of his Tesla.

Once inside, I checked my coat and looked around the interior of Felderman Hall. It had tall ceilings, a mosaic on the floor in the lobby, and an elegant vibe. If I was a betting woman, I'd lay money that the university development staff started using this space for courting donors as soon as the building was completed.

I said hello to the student working at the reception table, found my nametag, and gave myself a quick pep talk. Thanks to Cleo, I looked good. I was here as a guest of one of the stars of the night, a man who had already made his name and his fortune in tech in California. Even if I spilled red wine on the university president's white shirt, Grove University would still be thrilled to have Sam as part of its faculty. And how many donor events had I successfully navigated in my museum career? A bunch of stuffy academics couldn't be that much different.

Despite my positive self-talk, nerves danced in my stomach. I really, really wanted to make a good impression tonight. Because tonight mattered to Sam. And Sam—perhaps more than I might be willing to admit—mattered to me.

"There you are!" A Black woman wearing a hot pink dress and a turquoise pashmina approached me, carrying a very full glass of white wine. "You have to be Libby."

"Dallas?"

"That's me." She pulled me into a hug and then began talking at top speed. "I am so glad you're here tonight. And so glad Sam's finally dating someone. I tried like seven times to set him up with someone, but he was never interested. Of course, now I see why, if he was waiting for a woman as gorgeous as you." She paused for only a fraction of a second, not long enough for most people to inhale, and kept going. "Now we're not going to talk about that horrible murder, because I imagine people ask you about that everywhere you go these days, but I can't wait to hear all about the museum."

I blinked at her. "Um, uh, thank you."

She glanced down at my hands. "No wine? Come on, let's get you a drink. There might be, oh, I don't know"—

she tipped her head back and forth—"three or four boring speeches tonight. You may need alcohol to get through them."

With that, she took my arm and gestured to a bar set up in the corner of a large banquet room.

We strolled over, and I asked for red wine.

Dallas told the bartender to pour generously, which he did, and she led me to my seat, where I put down my purse. She switched two place cards at the table so that we were seated side by side and then introduced me to her husband and the provost, both of whom proved easy to talk to.

"I'm stealing her away for a while, Dallas," Sam said as he walked up. "Want to say hello to Mortimer?" He gestured across the room, where Mortimer Townsend was chatting with someone. I knew Mortimer as a member of the museum board, but he was here because of his day job, dean of the college of arts and science.

"Oh, yes." A familiar face was a very welcome sight.

Halfway across the room Sam stopped and whispered in my ear. "I actually wanted a minute alone with you so I could tell you something."

I looked at him.

"You are, by far, the most gorgeous woman in the room."

My cheeks grew hot, and my chest felt like a hundred fireflies were flitting about inside. "Thank you."

"What did you think of Dallas?" Sam grinned at me.

"A force of nature?" I said. "She makes Cleo seem shy."

Sam laughed. "She does indeed. I never met a woman who could talk that fast. It's like she doesn't need air."

I turned to him. "I know. How does she do that?"

"No idea, but she's a hoot. And a wonderful person. She's a surgical nurse at the hospital. I thought you'd enjoy meeting her this evening."

"That was really considerate of you."

"All part of the deal," he said. "And I do want to introduce you to several of my colleagues."

We said hello to Mortimer, met some of Sam's colleagues and their spouses, and sat down as the salads were served.

For an evening I'd been nervous about, the Grove University faculty awards banquet was truly a delight. Everyone I met was nice and easy to talk to, and I couldn't have been prouder of Sam, who was one of three faculty honored for exceptional teaching after being nominated by the students.

During dessert, while there was a lull in the program, Dallas asked me to tell her about my work at the museum. "Especially that famous painting by Clayton Smithton," she added.

I glanced over at Sam. He was engaged in a conversation with another faculty member, so the story was all mine to tell.

"A couple of years ago, when Sam first moved to Dogwood Springs, he purchased a home originally built by my ancestors, a place called Ashlington, out on Red Barn Road."

"Ooh, I know that house," Dallas said. "It's lovely."

Even though it wasn't in the family anymore, a ripple of

pride ran through me. "At the time, Ashlington was owned by one of my mother's sisters, my Aunt Gloria. She wanted to retire farther south, so she sold the house, and not long after he moved in, Sam found a painting in the attic that looked like a family—a mother, a father, and a daughter."

"Just sitting there in the attic?"

"No, it was way in the back of a closet under the eaves."

Dallas nodded.

I continued. "Sam contacted my aunt and told her that he thought he'd found a valuable work of art. He offered to give it back to her, but Aunt Gloria refused to be bothered with it. She'd already moved on, and once she makes up her mind…"

Dallas laughed. "I've got a family member like that."

"Then you understand," I said. "So, Sam showed the painting to me, wanting to donate it to the museum. The signature seemed authentic, and the people in the painting looked right, but I was suspicious of some of the historical details in the background. When an expert examined it, we learned that the original portrait had been altered. Someone had painted another girl out of the picture."

Dallas's eyes lit. "That's right! I heard there was a mystery girl."

"She's not a total mystery at this point, but we do want to learn more about her. Her name was Ivy Whitfield." I scooted forward in my seat, eager to share what we'd learned most recently. "A few years after the painting was done, Ivy was killed. She was alone one night at her father's bank here in town and was murdered by a robber. Sam and

I found her gravestone in the local cemetery, but we still don't know why she was painted out of the portrait."

"You're trying to figure it out, though, aren't you?"

"We are. At this point I'm hoping that the publicity we generated helps someone in town remember something a parent or grandparent may have told them about the girl who died in the bank robbery."

"Well, now I have to come in to see the painting," Dallas declared. "I want to know what Ivy looks like."

"Come by any time. The museum reopens tomorrow."

"I will," Dallas promised.

At last, after the program ended with an inspiring slideshow, Sam and I said good night to everyone at our table. We made our way to the lobby and, after I'd retrieved my coat, I waited in the entryway, watching for him to bring the car around and skimming through my email.

One email in particular caught my eye.

"I'm sorry, but I've got to finish reading this," I said as I climbed in the car.

Sam told me to take my time, navigated his way out of the university area, and started toward my house.

After a moment or two, I shut off my phone and squeezed it into my little purse. "You're never going to believe what I learned."

"That computer scientists are not nerdy at all, but totally the cool kids?"

I bit my lip. "Well, there was that one colleague of yours who talked for twenty minutes straight about his research."

Sam brushed my comment aside. "Ignore him. He's an anomaly."

I laughed. "Honestly, I had a marvelous time, and I was so proud to be there with you when you were honored."

Sam glanced over at me at a stop sign, and his eyes gleamed with pride. "I'm glad you enjoyed it. I appreciate you going with me." He gave me a smile that made my heart race. "But what did you really learn?"

"As I was waiting for you to bring the car around, I checked my email. I got a message from a woman in town who was cleaning out her attic. She found a trunk of things that belonged to one of her ancestors, a girl named Emily, who died from pneumonia in 1905. There's a photo in the trunk, and on the back, it says it's of Emily and her best friend."

Sam pulled into my driveway and came around to open my car door.

I climbed out and we walked toward my front porch. "Would you like to take a guess what her friend's name was?"

Sam drew in a breath. "Ivy Whitfield?"

"Got it in one," I said. "The woman said she and her husband are going to loan the trunk to the museum so that we can see if there is anything in it with information about Ivy."

"Fantastic!" Sam picked me up and spun me around.

Laughter bubbled out of me.

Then he lowered me until my feet landed gently on the

porch with the rest of my body pressed up against him, and he looked down at me.

My laughter stopped.

My breath grew shallow.

My heart fluttered.

And for a long moment, we stood there, gazing into each other's eyes.

Then he kissed me, slowly and tenderly, as if my kisses were as essential to his life as breathing.

When we stepped apart, I felt dazed, as if my brain had been shaken, allowing one particular thought to come to the top...

What my heart was saying about Sam.

Chapter Eleven

THE NEXT DAY WAS THURSDAY, Leap Day, our first day back in the museum after the murder, and the day Alice and I planned to talk to Emmett over lunch.

I brought in a box of treats from the donut shop for the staff and volunteers at the museum, but realized, after I put the box on the conference room table, that I wasn't very comfortable eating in a building where someone had recently been poisoned.

I found some disinfectant under the conference room sink, scrubbed the table, and washed my hands twice. I even put a little note by the treat box so people would know I'd been careful. I mean, I know Detective Harper said the museum was safe. I didn't expect cyanide to be dusted all over the furniture. But I still couldn't shake my paranoia.

Hopefully, in time, it would ease. I selected a sour cream cake donut and carefully placed it on a napkin.

Upstairs, I peered into the room where Brittany had

died. Other than the fact that the rug was gone, it didn't look much different from before the reception.

We'd had a crime committed at the museum once before and dealt with fingerprint powder. This time, I supposed, the only thing the police dusted for prints had been the wine bottle and the glass. All the suspects were identified. It didn't really matter who had rested their hand on a doorknob or on the mantel of the fireplace.

Anyway, despite my paranoia, I was grateful to be back at work.

I was in the upstairs hall when Rodney arrived and asked about the investigation.

I told him that Alice and I had plans to talk to a suspect over lunch, but with the tension I saw around Rodney's eyes, what Alice and I were doing didn't feel like enough. If Emmett was guilty, both Paula and Rodney would be devastated. I suddenly felt bad for having so much fun last night with Sam.

After I assured Rodney I would do my best, I hurried to my office, carefully set my donut on the napkin on the corner of my desk and called the woman who had emailed me about the trunk.

When she answered, I learned that in the wee hours of the morning she'd gotten a call from her daughter, who had gone into labor three weeks before her due date. Mom and Dad were already in Springfield, two hours away, and wouldn't be able to get the trunk to the museum until they came back to Dogwood Springs.

I did my best to hide my disappointment, thanked the

woman for being willing to let us look through the trunk when she returned, and said I hoped that everything went well with the baby.

Then I sank down in my chair, stared up at the ceiling, and eventually, grabbed my donut.

The donut was tasty, but it couldn't fully ease the double disappointment of feeling that I was failing Rodney and having to wait to learn more about Ivy. And I got so much glaze on my hands that I had to go to the bathroom to rinse them off. When I returned, I texted Sam with the news. Our investigation into Ivy would have to wait.

As I expected, attendance at the museum was low that morning, with low equaling zero guests. To be honest, after someone had been poisoned on the premises, I didn't expect things to pick up until the murderer was caught. I spent the time drafting an email to our major donors, struggling to explain what had happened. If they hadn't already heard, it wasn't the easiest news to break.

Finally, eleven o'clock rolled around. Alice and I had decided that I should take my lunch break early if we hoped to "accidentally" run into Emmett at the Hilltop Bed and Breakfast. The B & B didn't serve lunch. If we waited until noon, he might not be around.

The Hilltop was right outside Dogwood Springs and was one of the nicest establishments around. It was a white farmhouse, two and a half stories tall, set back from the road with trees in all directions.

Earlier in the morning, I'd shared our plan with Faye, and she said she'd ask the maid to clean Emmett's room at eleven. More often than not, Faye said, guests wandered down to the lobby to have another cup of coffee rather than listen to the vacuum cleaner.

I'd stayed at the B & B when I came to town for my interview, so I knew how restful the lobby was with its golden oak furnishing, soft blue carpeting, tan leather couches, and the faint aromas of delicious breakfasts and tasty afternoon cookies Faye served.

Sure enough, when Alice and I went inside, we saw Emmett sitting on one of the leather couches, dressed in a gray flannel plaid shirt and jeans, and rubbing his blond beard as he read something on his phone.

Alice and I walked closer, and he looked up.

"Well, hello," I said, mentally rehearsing the story Alice and I had agreed on as the pretext for our visit. "Alice and I are picking up Faye to take her to a Chamber of Commerce event. I think we're a little early. Do you mind if we join you here?"

"Please, sit." Emmett gestured to the other couch.

Alice was a good actress. She gave a respectable impression of awkwardness, fussed with her purse, then glanced over at Emmett. "How are you doing? This has all been such a shock."

He looked surprised, as if he'd forgotten all about Brittany's death. "Oh, I'm all right."

"I'm actually glad I ran into you. I love Dogwood Springs, but"—I shifted in my seat, trying to act embarrassed—"the people here are terrible gossips. I heard someone talking the other day and felt sure they were spreading a rumor, but I didn't know what to say to set them straight."

He set down his phone. "What did you hear?"

I lowered my voice. "I think it's pretty well gotten around town that Brittany was trying to convince Cordell to change his will. Given how wealthy he is, people seem to think everyone in the family had some degree of motive for killing her."

Emmett gave a half shrug. I guess when a man had as much money as Cordell, his family expected such speculation.

"Anyway," I continued. "They said that you're a research chemist and that, of all the people who were at the reception, it was most likely that you killed Brittany because you'd know how to handle a chemical like cyanide."

Emmett stiffened. "Who said that?"

I feigned trying to remember. "I don't really recall. It was someone at the café… But it seems wrong for people to be spreading gossip like that about you just because you're a scientist…"

He sat up taller, hands on his thighs, elbows askew. "If you hear anyone else saying I was the murderer, you can tell them that being a research chemist pays well. I don't need Grandpa's money, and I had no reason to kill Brittany. I wasn't even upstairs until after I heard all the commotion when she died."

"You weren't?" Now that I thought about it, I didn't remember seeing him early that evening.

He tugged at one of the cuffs of his flannel shirt and

shot me a sheepish look. "I imagine you worked hard to set it up, but I hate events like that reception where I have to talk to lots of people. So I put off going upstairs as long as possible by looking at the displays downstairs." He rubbed his hands along his thighs. "I hope that's okay. I didn't touch anything, and I turned the lights off as I left each room."

"Of course it's okay. We encourage people to view the exhibits." I grinned. What he'd done seemed like such a nerdy, scientist thing to do—avoiding the social event and looking at museum exhibits instead.

Alice rested a hand on her chin. "So you hadn't been upstairs at all before Brittany died?"

"No, ma'am," he said.

"Then there's no way you poisoned her," Alice said firmly. "I wonder who did..." She let her words trail off, like an angler dragging a lure through the water, waiting for Emmett to pounce on the idea and, hopefully, give us a clue.

It worked as well as the biggest, fattest worm around.

Emmett glanced around the lobby, then looked over at me. "If I were you, Libby, and I heard people speculating about who the murderer was, I'd suggest you consider Leah."

"Leah?" Alice and I asked together.

"You know about the wedding, right?" he asked in a low voice.

Alice and I exchanged confused looks.

Emmett continued. "Leah never got over the divorce, and she really, really hated Brittany for stealing Cordell away. She crashed their wedding and tried to stop it. You know the whole 'Does anyone have a reason why these two people should not marry' bit?"

Alice and I nodded.

"Leah stood up and started spouting off all sorts of stuff about Brittany only marrying Grandpa for his money." Emmett gave us a pointed stare.

"Whoa," I said. "That does make Leah look suspicious. Cordell and Brittany only married, what, about a year ago?"

"A year in April." Emmett pulled a vibrating phone from his jeans pocket. "Excuse me," he said. "This is work. I need to go upstairs to take this call."

Alice and I sat quietly as he trotted up the big staircase to the second floor. Then we found Faye and told her about our lie about the Chamber of Commerce. I suggested that if she ran into Emmett, she should mention that at the last minute she was unable to attend because of a crisis in the kitchen.

Then, reluctantly, Alice and I left the B & B.

She was due at the food pantry for a volunteers' meeting, and I had to get back to the museum to take a call from a potential donor at noon.

But as soon as possible, I wanted to come back to talk to Leah.

Chapter Twelve

I DROVE HOME, let Bella out, reheated some leftover enchiladas, and raced back to the museum just in time for my call.

Not surprisingly, the potential donor, a woman who'd grown up in Dogwood Springs and now lived in Florida, was not nearly as interested as she once had been in contributing to the museum. She'd heard all about the murder from a friend who lived locally. I did my best to convince her that the museum would bounce back after the tragedy, but I don't think I succeeded. I wasn't about to ask for a firm commitment, knowing I'd get a 'no,' so I simply wished her a good day and told her I'd contact her in the future.

With a sigh, I went down the main stairs. I'd take a quick loop around the first floor to stretch my legs, then pick out another treat and go back to my office. With luck, there would still be a cinnamon bun left.

To my surprise, the museum had a guest. Nick Calhoun stood by the front desk, chatting with a volunteer.

"Hi, Libby," he said. "I took you up on your invitation to come to the museum. I'm really enjoying it."

"I'm glad." Pride swelled in my chest. After all, Nick lived in Nashville, which had several large, well-respected history museums.

"I was excited to see the painting by Clayton Smithton. It's a nice piece, and the mystery attached to it only makes it more interesting. Any more clues about why that girl was painted out of the portrait?"

"Not yet." I told him about the letters in the trunk and about how we were going to have to wait to learn more.

He seemed almost as frustrated as I was, which in a weird way made me happy. If a random guest was intrigued by Ivy, then once we learned what was in those letters, it was bound to create even more interest in the painting and, once the murderer was caught, it might bring visitors back to the museum.

Nick turned toward the display rooms on the other side of the building, and I went to the conference room, found a cinnamon bun, and took it up the back service stairs to my office.

I had just made a trip to the bathroom to get the sugar off my hands when Leah came toward me in the hall.

What was she doing at the museum, and more importantly, what was she doing upstairs? Until we got that elevator, all the display space was on the first floor. And how did she manage to sneak past the volunteer at the check-in desk at the bottom of the main stairs?

"Libby? I tried to catch you before you left the bed-and-breakfast, but I missed you. The woman at the desk said you were in your office." She glanced at the nameplate by my door and tipped her head toward it. "Could I speak with you privately?"

"Uh, sure." But, with what I'd learned about the scene she made at Cordell and Brittany's wedding and her possible motive for killing Brittany, that door was staying open in case I needed to call for help.

I sat down behind my desk, tossed the sticky napkin from my cinnamon bun into the trash can, and tried to appear composed. "How can I help you?"

Leah took a moment, settling into the guest chair across from my desk. The last time I'd seen her, she'd been pale, suffering the effects of a panic attack. Today, she once again looked tan and fit, easily ten years younger than I knew her to be. Her dark hair had an effortlessly casual look that Cleo would approve of, and her navy knit pants, T-shirt, and running jacket probably cost more than my best dress clothes.

She rested one perfectly manicured hand on my desk. "I overheard you talking with Emmett back at the bed-and-breakfast. I wanted to set the record straight."

Her tone didn't sound threatening, and I relaxed a little. "Go on."

"I admit, I was devastated when Cordell divorced me to be with Brittany. I don't know if you can understand, but I was totally blindsided." A flash of vulnerability shot through her eyes.

Memories of my own divorce pinched at my chest. "I can. I got divorced a couple of years ago. It wasn't my idea."

"Then you do understand. For a while, I was stunned, unable to understand how Cordell could throw away what we had for that—that—that piece of trash."

I raised an eyebrow.

"Oh, you think because Brittany had a law degree, she was some class act." Leah let out a sharp laugh. "Hardly. She was sharp enough, but her law degree came from some third-rate school down in Arkansas. I shouldn't say this, but I heard from the wife of one of the partners that Brittany only got the job at that elite firm because of her other assets." Leah looked pointedly down at her own breasts.

Interesting. On the other hand, I wouldn't be surprised if every time Leah said, "I shouldn't say this," she followed it with a catty comment.

"Anyway, it was bad enough Cordell wanted to divorce me, but for him to marry a woman like that?" Leah let out a long sigh. "I'll admit I went a little nuts at the wedding, but I didn't kill her." She fanned out her fingers, then clasped her hands together. "A year ago, I might have. Now... Well, I guess I've come to terms with it. Cordell made it clear he didn't want to be married to me. If he wanted to be with Brittany, he was the one who was going to have to put up with her."

Should I push Leah for more information? It felt a bit risky, but we were never going to solve this crime if I didn't take opportunities when they were presented to me. And the woman had walked right into my office. "Playing devil's advocate," I said, "you could be hiding something. For instance, you could have killed Brittany to keep her from convincing Cordell to change his will."

"Believe me, I've got nothing to hide." Leah ran a hand over the back of her neck. "And when Cordell and I divorced, I got a nice settlement. Equally important, Cordell recommended I keep using our financial adviser. Thanks to some amazing trades she made this past year for me, I'm very, very comfortable."

I had a gut feeling that Leah was lying about something, but what she said made sense. Cordell probably had a financial advisor who could take one dollar and turn it into ten.

I thought for a moment. If Emmett had told me that he suspected Leah, he might have told Detective Harper the same thing and, unlike me, the detective might have the authority to check her claims about how well off she was. "Have you told all this to the police?"

"I have. But after I heard Emmett talking to you, I wanted to tell you as well." She pursed her lips, and for a moment she sat there, playing with the gold ring on her pinky, as if she wanted to say something more.

I kept my mouth shut, hoping my silence might nudge the words out of her.

She ran her hands down the legs of her pants. "Frankly, I think Emmett's trying to divert suspicion away from his mother.

"Heather?" I sat forward in my chair.

"Heather." Leah nodded. "Brittany was horrid to her, making fun of her for being overweight, saying the most awful things about the way Heather dressed."

I leaned back in my chair, evaluating what Leah said. This investigation seemed to be going back and forth like a game of tennis. Paula's branch of the family pushed the blame onto Leah's branch, and Leah's branch of the family sent it back.

"I know Heather didn't have a really classic style," Leah said. "But so what if she considered pink her signature color and wanted all of her dressy clothes to be floral and frilly?" Leah huffed out a breath. "It was her choice."

"I can't really see that Brittany could have said anything about Heather's clothes that was bad enough to lead to murder."

"You didn't hear what was said. Trust me, every drop of Brittany's nasty character came out when she attacked Heather. To be honest, if Heather did kill Brittany, someone should give her a medal for waiting as long as she did."

"Wow." I dropped my hands to my lap. "I don't know what to say."

"No need to say anything. I just thought you should know the truth, that I'm not a murderer." Leah rose, gave a prom queen wave, and left my office.

Quite the interesting visit. Were mean-girl comments enough to make a grown woman commit murder? I had my doubts.

But it wouldn't hurt to have a chat with Heather.

Chapter Thirteen

AFTER LEAH LEFT, I sat at my desk, trying to work. After fifteen minutes, I knew it was useless. Every time I tried to focus on something for the museum, all I could think about was the call I'd had with a potential donor earlier. Our budget required public support, but no one was ever going to contribute to the museum until the murderer was caught.

In the past, when I'd done some amateur sleuthing, I'd made sure to pursue any investigation on my own time. But solving this crime would be helping the museum. With only the slightest feeling of guilt, I scooped up my purse, told Imani I'd be gone for an hour or so, and drove back to the bed-and-breakfast, blasting my favorite music, '70s' rock and roll. Early, angry Billy Joel was perfect to psych myself up.

As soon as I parked, I hurried across the parking lot to the covered porch, then forced myself to calm down before I entered the building.

Inside, the lobby looked as restful as ever, but it was completely empty. How was I going to engineer an opportunity to talk to Heather? It was bad enough I'd come here on my own. Knocking on the woman's door and accusing her of murder didn't seem like a good plan.

I spotted Faye behind the counter in the gift shop and darted inside. Shelves displayed items from area artists, including silk floral arrangements that I knew were created by the hotel maid, as well as locally made jam, soap, and wine.

Faye stood at the counter, putting price tags on bars of handmade soap. Her hazel eyes lit when she noticed me. "Libby, what brings you back so soon?"

"Hi, Faye. I wanted to talk to Heather Ford. Have you noticed if she's left the B & B?" I caught a hint of the scent from one of the bars of soap, picked it up, and sniffed deeply. It smelled fantastic.

"I don't really keep track of my guests' comings and goings, but I haven't seen her." Faye used a fingernail to pry a particularly stubborn label off the sheet. "That bar of soap's fragrance is white tea and ginger, and it's made with goat's milk, so it's wonderful for your skin."

Possibly exactly what my poor hands needed after the slightly paranoid extra handwashing I'd been doing since the poisoning at the museum. I dug my wallet out of my big purse and asked Faye to ring up a bar. I'd make my purchase and casually sit in the lobby, answer email, and cross my fingers that Heather would appear.

A minute later, with my new soap tucked in my purse, I stepped out into the lobby.

My pulse quickened. Coming back to the B & B had worked!

Heather was coming down the stairs from the second floor, and her long blond curls glinted in the light. She was talking on her phone, telling her mom that she'd be waiting for her to pick her up and that she'd text Emmett and tell him to hurry up and get down to the lobby.

Absorbed in her phone call, she never even noticed me as she walked over to the couch facing the lobby door, sat down, and picked a bit of lint off her sweater.

I wandered over nonchalantly, as if I spent all my free time at the B & B, and stopped near her. "Heather! I was hoping I might see you." I sat down next to her on the couch.

She slid her phone into her purse and turned toward me. Her expression was pleasant, even if her eyes looked perplexed.

"When I'm not running the history museum, I do a bit of amateur sleuthing. After the police started thinking your mom might have killed Brittany, she asked me to see if I could learn who the real killer was."

The confusion cleared from Heather's eyes. "Thank heaven someone is considering other suspects. How can I help?"

"Well, I don't believe everything I'm told, but I do try to follow up, to be sure..." I bit my lower lip, doing my best to look uncomfortable. "So I thought I should ask. Someone said that you might have killed Brittany because she was rude to you."

"I can just imagine who would have said such a thing." Heather crossed her arms over her chest. "It was Leah, wasn't it? That woman always thinks the worst of me."

No way was I answering that. "Um, I shouldn't say, but is it true that Brittany said awful things about how you dress?" I gestured to Heather's sweater, which was cream with pale pink hearts intricately knit into it. A satin patch over her heart was embroidered with the words "Celebrate Valentine's *Month*." "Personally, I think that's darling." Not something I would ever wear, but very cute.

"Thank you." Heather straightened her sweater. "And yes, Brittany said horrible things about how I dressed and about me being overweight—as if I don't try to lose weight." She huffed out a breath. "I've tried every diet out there. Honestly, I don't have any idea why she had it in for me. I tried my best to be nice to her when she married Daddy."

"I can understand how her comments could make you angry." I said slowly.

"More hurt than angry, but yeah, they bothered me." Heather sighed. "But I certainly wasn't upset enough to kill her because of it. I wouldn't have a clue where to get cyanide, and I'd be afraid to use it. Besides, if I killed everyone who was rude to me because I'm overweight, I'd have killed dozens of people by now. Folks can be so thoughtless." She shook her head.

"I'm sorry." Something about the expression in her eyes, as if she felt that she'd never lose weight and would always have to endure rude comments, made my heart ache for her. Had I ever inadvertently been unkind to someone who was overweight? I didn't think so, but it wouldn't hurt to be especially sensitive in the future. "Thank you for talking with me."

"Not a problem. I appreciate that you're trying to help Mom, and I understand that you need to follow up every lead." She paused. A half second later, her mouth twitched.

Was there something she wanted to say? "Did you ... did you have a lead I should check into?"

"I hate to cast blame on someone who might be innocent." She wrapped a lock of hair around one finger. "But have you read anything about...?" She untangled her finger, then pulled her phone from her purse, tapped quickly on the screen, and held the phone toward me.

I leaned in closer to read the words.

She'd pulled up a website that looked trustworthy and found information about cyanide. The paragraph she pointed to discussed ways cyanide was used. I read it, thinking through each use and how it might relate to our suspects. Cyanide was used to make paper, plastics, and textiles—not really helpful. Photo developing—probably not involved since most people used the cameras on their phones for digital images. Mining—not relevant, from what I knew and—

Heather tapped the screen, drawing my eye to the last item on the list, jewelry manufacture.

Our eyes met.

"I wasn't really trying to pin the murder on someone

else," she said. "I didn't know much about cyanide, and so I looked it up online. You know what Brad does for a living, don't you?"

"I do." And I remembered how calm he seemed after the murder. Calmer than anyone else in the room. Was that because, as the killer, he wasn't shocked by the murder?

"I don't know if his company uses cyanide," Heather said. "But if you're looking into things, it might be worth checking."

"Can you send me a link to that page? I'd like to read more."

"Sure." She had me type my number into her phone.

The message made a whooshing sound and, deep in my purse, my phone dinged.

I thanked Heather and headed out to my car. I might be basing too much on gut instinct, but I didn't think Heather was a murderer. Unlike with Leah, I felt Heather had been honest with me.

And she'd given me another clue to follow.

Halfway to town, my phone dinged with another text. At the light on the edge of town, I dug my phone out of my purse and found a message from Imani.

The trunk from Ivy's friend arrived! The owner said he had to come back to town for a work meeting and had time to drop it off. Rodney and I put it in your office.

Chapter Fourteen

I GAZED down at the phone, excitement bubbling inside me. I couldn't wait to see what was inside that trunk!

To be fair, though, I shouldn't rummage through it the minute I got back to the museum. I should wait for Sam.

Still, as soon as I'd parked behind the museum, I raced up the back stairs to my office.

An antique steamer trunk sat on the floor in front of my desk. It had a rounded top, a latch with a key on the front, side clasps to secure it closed, and a decorated portion featuring a pattern of red flowers on a gold background.

I ran a hand over the top of it, and then, with enormous willpower, I stepped away and sat behind my desk. I sent a text to Sam, telling him the trunk had been delivered, and we made plans to meet after he finished at the university at five.

Luckily, work provided me with plenty of distractions the rest of the afternoon. A tiny trickle of visitors was coming to the museum, but the volunteer who was supposed to staff the gift shop was too nervous about the murder to come in, and, to make matters worse, she'd been spreading her anxiety to other volunteers. Imani was taking up the slack by covering the front desk and the gift shop. Which left Rodney and me to deal with the bird that managed to fly in the front door. We probably looked like some type of slapstick comedy routine trying to get it to fly out a window of the third-floor attic.

And to think that when I was in college, none of my professors ever discussed how to deal with a stubborn sparrow or how volunteers might be affected by a murder on the museum premises.

At five, I drove home and let Bella out. Sam met me there, and once Bella had eaten, we got in his car. While he drove the three of us to the museum, I told him what I'd learned from Heather, and he filled me in on how his classes were going and on his latest cooking project, learning to make a white sauce called béchamel from scratch. When I first met Sam, he told me he'd been learning to cook and had the kitchen at Ashlington remodeled. Lately, he seemed to be trying to further upgrade his skills to match the fancy kitchen.

Once we reached the museum, there was a bit of a delay in the parking lot when Bella spotted a squirrel in a nearby tree. Eventually, after a good deal of barking, the three of us went into the museum.

"Before I met you, Libby, I never imagined history could

be this exciting," Sam said as he followed Bella and me up the back stairs to my office.

"Remember, there's always a chance the trunk may not tell us anything more about Ivy. It may only have that one photo and old dresses that were packed away when Emily died." Personally, I loved historic clothing, but even I was hoping for more.

"Is the trunk locked?"

"Yes, but the man who brought it in also brought the key. He told Imani that it was in the lock when they found the trunk in the attic."

I unlocked my office, and Bella went right to the trunk, nose aquiver.

"Even she knows how cool this is," Sam said. He pulled my two guest chairs up on either side of the trunk and gestured to the key in the lock of the trunk. "You do the honors."

I sat, leaned down, and turned the key. For a lock that was more than a century old, it moved easily.

Sam opened the lid, letting out a faint smell that warmed my historian's heart, a mix of stale air and musty old papers. Inside the lid was a label identifying the trunk as manufactured by the F Endebrock Trunk Company of St. Louis.

The sectioned tray held a pair of tortoiseshell combs, four handkerchiefs, two pairs of long, leather gloves, a parasol, and a hat, decorated with lace and ribbon, that had once been a lovely rose color but had mostly faded. So far, nothing about Emily's best friend, Ivy.

Sam lifted out the tray.

Below it was a fox fur—the creepy kind that had the head attached—and a high-necked, rose-colored dress with a lace inset and slightly puffed, elbow-length sleeves. If the owners were willing to loan it to the museum, the dress would be a lovely addition to our display of historic clothing. Ordinarily, I'd have been thrilled to see a Victorian dress in such good condition, but I set it aside and dug deeper.

I lifted out two more dresses and a book of poetry by Keats, and then, under the book, I found four yellowed letters, tied together with a blue ribbon.

Sam and I exchanged glances.

The top letter had no envelope, simply Emily's first name written on the outside of the folded paper.

I carefully unfolded it, and Sam and I leaned in to read.

June 25, 1905

Dear Emmy,

I have no choice except to run away. I will try to write again, but please don't tell anyone that you heard from me because everyone is supposed to believe I am dead. You will always be my dearest friend.

It was unsigned, except for a sketch of a single ivy leaf.

For a half second, I stopped breathing. "It's from her." I pointed at the date. "June 25, 1905—that's the day Ivy was supposedly killed by a robber at her father's bank. At least that's what the article we found in the newspaper said."

"But she didn't die." Sam touched the letter. "She ran away."

My heart sped. I'd read about things historians had uncovered, but I'd never been involved in something this fascinating. I reached for the next letter, which was in an envelope addressed with Emily's full name and street address, the same address as the couple who'd found the trunk in their attic. It was postmarked St. Louis, June 27, 1905.

Sam pointed to the envelope. "Why doesn't it have a return address? Was Ivy trying to hide where she went?"

"Possibly, but in 1905, using a return address wasn't that common," I said. "Most people didn't use them until the 1960s."

Sam looked over at me. "I never knew that."

I stopped myself from mentioning how useful it was to have a knowledge of history and slid the second letter from the envelope.

June 26, 1905

Dearest Emmy,

I am so sorry I had to leave Silersville without telling you goodbye.

The last time I saw you, at the party, I wanted so much to speak with you, but I could not escape from Father and that horrid, ancient Willard Fore. I never dreamed that as soon as

I turned eighteen, Blanche would convince Father to pressure me to marry Mr. Fore, just to get access to his family money. How could she even think such a thing? It is not the 1700s! And I cannot believe that they sprung the engagement on me as a surprise, in front of dozens of people at a party. I'm certain that idea came from Blanche, as a way to force me to accept.

Somehow, at the time I managed to act so surprised that I could not give an answer.

After everyone went home, Father and Blanche and I had a horrible argument. They insisted that I must marry Mr. Fore, that his money was essential to save Father's bank. In desperation, I even offered to let them sell Mama's jewelry, which she promised on her deathbed was to be mine. Blanche said the jewelry wasn't worth nearly enough money and that I must marry. I refused, and finally, a day later when we were still arguing, I said that before I would marry that man, I would take Mama's jewelry and run away.

Oh, Emmy, I know I won't be able to describe Blanche's expression well enough for you to picture it. Her eyes grew small and hard, and her mouth tightened. She stared at me for a moment and then drew herself up taller and calmly said that if I left town, I must never, ever return.

I'd heard the expression about a person's blood running cold, but before that moment, I never knew it could actually happen. In that instant, though, I understood. I realized nothing good would ever come for me in Silersville, not as long as Blanche was my stepmother.

And so I told Blanche and Father that I would take the train out of town early the next morning.

Blanche stopped me in the middle of a sentence. She said Mr. Fore might hear of me being at the train station, learn where I had gone, and follow me. Instead, she said I should ride my little mare, Buttercup, ten miles away to the town of Rolla, change my appearance as best I could, and take the train from there. I could scarcely believe it. She wanted me to leave town like a criminal!

Father protested, but she glared at him, and he became silent.

Emmy, my hands were shaking so hard that I could barely pack, but I bundled up Mama's jewelry, some dresses, a nightgown, and a few small things, and I took them to the barn.

I was slipping back into the house to say goodbye to Father when I overheard him talking with Blanche and learned the truth.

I beg of you, Emmy, do not breathe a word of this. I'm horribly ashamed to tell you, but Father had gambled away not only our family money but also much of the money deposited in his bank. Without the funds Mr. Fore would contribute to the bank when we married, Father's actions would surely be discovered.

The minute I said I would run away, my scheming stepmother came up with a plan. They would invent a robbery and tell everyone I was dead, shot by a ne'er-do-well who took money from the bank. Blanche's brother, who runs the funeral home, could help them pull off the deception. Father's embez-

zling from the bank would be hidden, and with luck, Willard might still agree to invest in my memory.

And Father agreed to all of this.

Tears ran down my face, and I turned and walked back to the barn without saying goodbye.

I rode Buttercup part way to Rolla until darkness fell and I was forced to stop and spend the night in the woods. I barely slept, terrified by strange noises. The next morning, I rode the rest of the way to Rolla and sold Buttercup to a man who worked at the livery stable and wanted a horse for his niece.

Then I arranged my hair and put on a hat with a veil to hide my face as much as possible. I used the money from selling Buttercup to book a seat on a train to St. Louis.

When we arrive in St. Louis, I will mail this letter, sell a bit of Mama's jewelry, and board another train. I have no idea where I'm going, but some of my fellow passengers have told me about the yellow fever scares, so I know at least one direction to avoid.

Please do not tell anyone, especially Willard Fore, that you heard from me.

I am determined to make a new future for myself, one where I can make my own decisions. I pray I will find good people, people far kinder than my stepmother, and perhaps, if I am lucky, I will find a friend almost as dear as you.

Like the first letter, the second was signed with the same drawing of a single ivy leaf, stem pointing diagonally up and to the left.

"Wow." I sat the second letter on my lap. "That whole newspaper article we read was based on lies."

"I should have realized there was something fishy about that article when I read it," Sam said.

"Why?"

"Don't you remember? Her father said that when he found her body, he called his brother-in-law, who ran the funeral home. They didn't call the sheriff until after the brother-in-law had supposedly taken away Ivy's body. But think about it. If someone you loved had been killed, the first thing you'd do would be to call the sheriff so the killer could be caught."

I stared at him. "You're right. That's how they hid the fact that there was no body."

"Yep. And now we know why she was painted out of the portrait," Sam said. "Her stepmother hated her."

"But we still don't know where Ivy went." I slid the next letter out of the envelope. "At least not yet."

Sam moved his chair closer, and we began to read.

July 17, 1905

Dearest Emmy,

I will begin teaching school in the fall. I cannot believe how fortunate I am to have found a path for my new life so easily! I have jumped ahead too far, though. First, I should tell you what has happened since my last letter.

In St. Louis, I sold one of Mama's necklaces, a jet one that was never her favorite, and then I boarded another train. I was searching for my compartment when I collided with a little girl with adorable blond curls.

When her mother asked what brought me on the train, I spoke without thinking. "I'm running away because my stepmother was forcing me to marry a man I don't love. I'm going as far away as I can, and I'm going to find my own future."

As soon as I said it, I covered my mouth in horror and closed my eyes.

My honesty paid off, though, because the woman burst into laughter. "Bully for you!" she cried. And just like that, I had a new friend, Ida Anderson.

At dinner that evening, Ida's husband asked about my education. Their town's teacher had recently eloped, and he was president of the school board. By the time we went to sleep that night, I had a job, and I knew exactly where I was headed.

I am now boarding with a dear widow woman who owns a dress and shirt shop. As soon as she saw how little I arrived with, she began knitting me mittens for the winter. She even offered to loan me money to buy wool to make winter dresses. I told her that I had some resources but hadn't been able to take much with me when I traveled. She has helped me tremendously with sewing winter dresses, especially with my buttonholes. You know how I always struggled with them. I think she enjoys having someone to fuss over. She has a son, but he is grown and lives on a farm, and I have not yet met him.

I am happy here, Emmy, but I miss you. I so desperately wish I could talk with you.

I hope you still collect your family's mail. In case you don't, I won't write often. I do not know how you could explain these letters to your parents.

There was a postscript, but all we could see was the "P.S." The bottom of the letter, including the signature, was damaged and unreadable.

Sam and I exchanged glances.

"It's her, though," I said. "It's the same story and the same handwriting."

"But it doesn't say where she went," he said.

"Let's check the postmark." I pulled out the envelope.

"Oh, man." Sam pointed. "It's mostly on top of the stamp and so faint you can't read it."

He was right. Even when we held the envelope under my desk lamp, the postmark was impossible to read.

We sat back down, and I quickly opened the last letter, which had no envelope.

December 18, 1905

Dear Emmy,

Did you guess from the handwriting that the letter was from me, even though the name on the envelope was different? I married Thomas, the son of the woman I was boarding with! I know in my last letter, the one where I sent you my address in town, I told you how I met him. He is such a good man. He won my heart almost the first day we met and had only been calling on me for two months when he asked me to marry him. Emmy, I knew, I just knew deep in my heart that there was no reason to have a long engagement. Thomas is the man I was meant to marry.

"Wait," Sam said. "Where's the letter where she sent her address?"

"Only these four were tied with the ribbon." I set them on my desk. "Let's see if it's somewhere else in the trunk."

We took everything out of the trunk and set it on my desk, but we only found more clothing, a lovely pair of dancing slippers, and some boots.

No missing letter.

I blew out a long breath, and we went back to the last letter we had.

After Thomas's father passed away, his mother moved to town to open her dress shop, and Thomas took over the family dairy. Thank goodness two of his cousins help us with the milking, bottling, and delivering. It's far too big a job for Thomas and me alone.

I could not ask for a sweeter husband or a more charming mother-in-law. That dear woman even created my wedding dress. I sometimes think she began planning our wedding the minute she met me.

I did not tell anyone except Thomas about how Father stole from the bank, but his mother, the rest of the family here, and my close friends know I ran away to avoid marrying someone I didn't love. I assumed they would all disapprove, but they didn't. Thomas says a lot of people are running from something or searching for something.

I am no longer running. I have found all I could ever seek.
Please write back soon.
Your friend,

Once again, it was signed with the same ivy leaf.

"Wow." I sat back in my chair. "What a story."

Sam nodded, then his eyes narrowed. "You said Emily died in 1905 of pneumonia. When in 1905 did she die?"

I picked up the newspaper obituary from the tray that had been at the top of the trunk. "November 4, 1905." I looked again at Ivy's last letter, which was dated mid-December. "So Emily never received this. She died before it arrived."

"The letter with Ivy's address wasn't with the others," Sam said. "What do you bet that Emily's mother opened that last letter Ivy sent, found the other letters, and wrote to Ivy to let her know Emily died?"

I pictured Emily's mother, getting a letter addressed to her daughter a month after her death. If it had been me, I'd have opened it. "I bet you're right. And she kept Ivy's secret, possibly as a way to honor her daughter's memory. Oh, that poor woman, losing her daughter, and poor Ivy, learning her friend died." I let out a sigh. "But death from pneumonia wasn't all that uncommon back then. We don't realize today how much antibiotics changed our lives."

Sam dipped his chin in acknowledgement. "These letters might explain why we couldn't find Ivy Whitfield in the 1910 census," Sam said. "She was married by that point. Would the census takers have asked her maiden name in 1910?"

"I don't think so." I sat for a moment, thinking about Emily and Ivy. "I'm sad about Emily, but I just love that Ivy built a whole new life for herself."

"Me too. In spite of having a stepmother who wanted to marry her off for money, in spite of a father who was a gambler and a thief, she found friends and a job and a family."

"She did." Life in the early 1900s was hard, but Ivy was proof that a person could start over and build the life they wanted.

Then, as now, new beginnings were possible. Look at Alice, going back to school in her fifties. Look at me, starting over in Dogwood Springs after my divorce.

"I still wish we knew Thomas's last name or where Ivy ended up. I'd like to know more about Ivy's life." I tapped the stack of letters. "We do know one thing, though. She didn't go south when she left St. Louis."

Sam's brow furrowed. "How do we know that?"

"Because of the comment about yellow fever. There was a big yellow fever epidemic in New Orleans in the summer of 1905."

"See," Sam took my hand. "You've already found another clue." He stood, gently pulled me to stand in front of him, and wrapped his arms around me. Then he threaded his fingers into the hair at the back of my neck. "You're amazing, Libby." He gazed into my eyes and lowered his lips to mine.

My heart pounded, and I returned his kiss and slid closer into his arms.

Inch by inch, his lips wandered to a tender spot at the base of my ear. His kisses lingered there and then worked their way slowly down my neck.

My chest filled with warmth, and I had tingles all over and—

Bella barked and nudged my leg.

I pulled back from Sam, laughing. "Someone," I said as I rubbed Bella's ears, "feels left out."

Sam grinned down at Bella. "Then how about we pick up some dinner from that Mexican place you love, take it back to your apartment, and spend some time discussing where Ivy might have gone, talking about Heather's theory that Brad killed Brittany, and telling Bella how wonderful she is?"

"Sounds perfect." I'd eaten enchiladas for lunch, but I'd never turn down tacos.

We packed everything but the letters into the trunk and left the museum. Back at my place, we didn't come to any brilliant conclusions, but the two of us—and Bella—did have a lovely evening.

Chapter Fifteen

THE NEXT DAY was the first day of March, a bright, sunny day in the fifties when Cordell should have been out trout fishing, filled with pride after a week of basking in the adoration and gratitude of Dogwood Springs. Instead, the poor man had told everyone he had no interest in fishing because his heart was far too heavy. According to Rodney, Brittany would be cremated, and a memorial service held in Nashville in a month, when her grandfather would hopefully be recovered from a recent illness and able to attend with the rest of her family from Arkansas. In the meantime, the mayor was holding a small, subdued reception in his office today, a time when the organizations that had been scheduled to receive donations from Cordell could pay their respects to the family.

With the mayor's reception in mind, I put on a black dress, black heels, and my pearls, just as I would if I was going to a funeral. I filled Bella's water bowl with fresh water and was about to walk out the door to the reception when Sam texted.

He'd checked online to see if Brad's jewelry manufacturing company used any processes that required cyanide.

It did.

And—equally interesting—Sam had learned that Brad's company was failing, desperately in need of cash, giving him not only means and opportunity but also a strong motive for killing Brittany. If she was out of the way, it was bound to be easier for Brad to convince Cordell to help him save his company.

Luckily, all of Cordell's family was expected at the mayor's reception, and Alice would be there as well. The two of us could talk to Brad.

I thanked Sam for the information and drove to city hall.

On the way, my phone dinged with a text. Once I parked, I saw it was from Rodney. The police had arrested Paula. He didn't go on and on about it, but I knew Rodney and could read between the lines. He was worried sick.

Once I reached city hall, I found room 207, the room where city council meetings were held. A raised dais held a table and two chairs, and the main level had rows of seating. Alice stood on the far side of the room.

I hurried over and whispered as quietly as I could to fill her in on Paula's arrest and what Sam had learned about Brad's business. Like me, Alice was frustrated by Paula's arrest and even more determined to figure out the killer. The two of us made a plan to "casually" bump into Brad at the end of the event and ask a subtle question or two. We were just firming up the details of what we'd say when the mayor asked us all to take our seats.

Forty-five minutes later, Dogwood Springs's top elected official was still droning on about how proud the entire town was of Cordell.

One of my legs had fallen asleep, and I squirmed, trying to stretch it out without looking obvious. Emmett, who was sitting in front of me, must have been nodding off because his head repeatedly sank lower, then jerked up. Even Cordell, who sat beside the mayor at the table on the dais, seemed bored with hearing how wonderful he was.

Finally, the mayor stopped talking. The locals filed past Cordell and the rest of the family like a receiving line, expressing their admiration of Cordell and their sympathy for the loss of Brittany. The comments about Cordell rang with sincerity. People were proud of the local boy who'd made such a success of himself. The comments about Brittany were more forced. I overheard more than one person mentioning how beautiful she had been. After all, what else could politely be said about the woman?

As Alice and I were slipping out the door, hoping to talk to Brad in the hall, the mayor intercepted us with questions about attendance at the museum.

"It's been low," I said, edging toward the door.

"I expect it will stay low until the whole situation is resolved," Alice added.

Though we tried to slip away, the mayor gave us what sounded like a canned speech about his confidence in the police and how the situation should be resolved soon.

When Alice and I at last escaped, we dashed down the stairs only to see Brad riding away in a silver sports car driven by Leah.

"He's probably headed back to the B & B." I gestured to my car, and Alice and I got in.

I wasn't a Dogwood Springs native, of course, but I'd lived in the area long enough to have learned a few short cuts. I cut through an alley and took a back road to the B & B that—as long as a driver didn't get behind a truck from the quarry—was faster than the highway.

Luck was with us, and there were no quarry trucks on the road. When we arrived at the bed-and-breakfast, Leah's car was parked in the lot, and although she must have gone inside, Brad was still in the car, reading something on his phone.

I pulled into the space next to Leah's car.

"Alice," I said. "Look over out of the corner of your eye and tell me when he's getting out." I used the pretext of digging in my purse for something to cover our delay in leaving the car.

"Now!" she cried.

The two of us scrambled out, doing our best to appear nonchalant as we hurried to catch up to Brad, whose long legs quickly covered the ground.

"Oh, hello," Alice said. "Such a nice event this morning, wasn't it?" She beamed at him. "Your father is Dogwood Springs's biggest success story. You must be very proud."

"Yes, of course." Brad's tone was convincing, but he glanced toward the B & B.

"I heard that you're quite a success as well." I did my best to sound enthusiastic despite the fact that I knew his company was failing. "You run a jewelry business?"

He turned back toward me. "I do. My wife, Kelly, is the designer, and I handle the manufacturing." His steps slowed, and his chest swelled.

Typical. He was a lot more interested in talking about how wonderful he was than about how wonderful his father was.

"We do a lot of business online," he said. "Kelly G's Jewelry. You may have heard of us."

Kelly G's? That was his company? "I have heard of that. I had a friend back in Philadelphia who ordered from your website all the time." I had to admit, it was good costume jewelry. "Nice pieces. They were stylish, but not so trendy that you'd think they would quickly go out of fashion."

Brad's eyes shone. "Thank you. I'll tell my wife you said that."

"But..." Alice bit her lip, doing her best thoughtful look. "Didn't I read somewhere that jewelry manufacturers use all sorts of dangerous chemicals, including cyanide?"

The light in Brad's eyes dimmed, and he sniffed. "Really, is that what this is all about? You're trying to pin Brittany's murder on me?" He drew himself up to look even taller and glared down at us in a way that made me glad I wasn't alone.

"I was simply making conversation," Alice said.

"Plee—ase." Brad shot her a look of disgust. "Don't insult my intelligence. It's none of your business, but yes, we use sodium cyanide at our plant, which is precisely why I couldn't be the killer."

Huh? Alice and I exchanged glances.

His nostrils flared. "Getting through this week with one mind-numbing event after another isn't easy. The night Brittany was killed, I had four shots of Scotch before I went to the museum. And"—his face reddened—"being someone who fully understands the toxicity of cyanide because we use it in our plant, there is no way, absolutely no way, that I would handle cyanide when I'd been drinking."

"Oh." That put things in a different light. When we'd waited for the police to finish their interviews after the murder, I'd thought Brad had looked relaxed, the most relaxed of anyone there. But he hadn't been merely relaxed, he'd been drunk. How much Scotch did he drink on a daily basis if he managed to seem so normal after four shots?

I opened my mouth to apologize, but Brad sniffed, spun on his heel, and strode toward the B & B.

Alice and I looked at each other. "That didn't go too well, did it?" she said.

"Not really. Do you believe him?"

Alice rubbed a hand over her chin, then nodded. "I do. If he was going to lie, I'd think he'd leave out how much he drinks."

"I agree." Even for someone who liked Scotch, four shots to get through a reception seemed excessive. "So we did learn something, but we still don't know who the killer is." I gestured toward the B & B. "Would you mind if we popped in? I'd like to update Faye on what we know at this point."

"Good idea." Alice continued walking toward the door. "As long as we don't have to talk to Brad. He may not be the killer, but I definitely made him mad."

"We'll steer well clear of him," I agreed.

Inside, we saw Brad on the far side of the room, headed into the dining room, where Faye kept coffee and a soft drink fountain available. He was far enough away that I felt comfortable going into the gift shop.

Faye greeted us from behind the counter. On impulse, I selected another bar of goat's milk soap, this time a vanilla mango scent, and took it to the register. No reason I couldn't buy a bar of soap while I filled her in.

Faye rang me up and handed me my change.

"Thanks, Faye. I wanted to tell you what we've—"

A scream pierced the air, followed by several loud thumps.

Faye, Alice, and I ran out of the gift shop and into the lobby.

Cordell lay crumpled at the base of the stairs, his face ashen, one leg bent in an unnatural angle.

My chest tightened. Oh, the poor man. Was he even alive?

"I'm calling 9-1-1." Alice already had her phone out.

Faye and I hurried to Cordell and knelt beside him.

He was alive, but his leg was clearly broken. His face was damp with perspiration, and he was trying to speak.

"Someone," he said so softly that I could barely hear him.

"No need to talk," Faye said. "Save your strength. An ambulance will be here soon."

He grabbed my arm and pulled, as if he wanted me to lean down.

I bent closer.

"Someone," he said again. "Pushed me."

His eyelids fell shut.

Chapter Sixteen

FAYE and I stared down at Cordell, looking for signs of life.

"He's still breathing," I said. "I can see his chest rising and falling."

"Thank goodness." Faye gestured toward Cordell's body. "I know we can't move him. Is there anything we can do for him while we wait for the ambulance?"

"I'd be afraid if we try to make him more comfortable, we might make things worse." I rested a hand lightly on his arm. "Hang in there, Cordell. Help is coming."

I didn't have the skills or equipment to help with his injuries, but the man had used what strength he had to tell me he'd been pushed. The least I could do was try to figure out who had pushed him. I scrambled to my feet and scanned the room.

At the top of the stairs, I caught a glimpse of Leah slipping away.

Leah—the same suspect who I'd thought lied to me.

Had she been cold-blooded enough to push Cordell down the stairs?

I edged closer to Alice and quietly asked her to make sure that the 9-1-1 operator knew we needed not only an ambulance but also the police.

Then I turned to Faye. "Do you think he fell the entire way down?"

"He did," Brad said. He had rushed over to join us, all signs of his earlier anger replaced with concern. "I was coming out of the dining room and saw the whole thing." Brad looked down at Cordell and pressed his lips together. "Poor Dad." He glanced toward the windows as if checking for the ambulance, then looked back at his father.

Given the distance from the hospital, the response time for the ambulance was probably fast. To me, though, it felt like hours.

Finally, the police arrived, and less than a minute later, the paramedics.

The paramedics rushed into action, but Detective Harper was more deliberate. First, he sent officers to secure the B & B. Then, he assembled every person in the building in the lobby and stationed an officer with us. Just as he'd done after Brittany had been killed, he spoke to each of us alone, with me last.

When I was led into the dining room where Detective Harper was interviewing witnesses, he gestured to the chair across from him, crossed one arm over his chest, and pressed his other fist against his mouth as if holding back a lecture—or an official warning. "You're just too stubborn to stop interfering, aren't you, Libby?"

"I was in the gift shop, buying soap," I protested.

"Um-hmm." His face twisted into an expression that combined disbelief and disgust. "I'm not even going to ask why a woman like you, who seems like she maintains regular office hours at the museum, was shopping here on a Friday afternoon."

That was a good question, but one I didn't want to answer. Which meant it was time for me to change the subject. "Will Cordell be okay?"

"He regained consciousness while the paramedics were treating him. He broke several bones, though, and he's turning seventy, right?"

I nodded.

"I'm sure he's headed for Columbia or St. Louis. At his age, his injuries are too serious for the Dogwood Springs Hospital to handle. Given what Faye and Alice told me he said after he fell, I'll make sure the police there keep him under protection."

"Good. Even in the hospital, he could be in danger."

The detective's jaw tightened. "As could anyone who sticks their nose into this case." He gave me a pointed stare. "This could easily have been a second murder."

My mouth went dry. Tangling with the Calhoun family was risky business. "At least the suspect list is getting shorter. There's no way that Brad could be the killer. He was in the dining room on the first floor. But I think I know who—"

Detective Harper's eyes hardened. "Libby, do you understand the meaning of the phrase 'stay out of this'? You are not a cop. You shouldn't even have a suspect list."

Of course I had a suspect list, and Leah was at the top of it. The detective needed to take her in for questioning. "But—"

His face grew red, and he stood up. "Enough. The more I talk to you, the more you interfere, and you're going to get hurt. I've already got a clear picture of what happened here. All I need now is for you to do one thing." He glared at me. "Stop. Playing. Detective."

Fine. I grabbed my purse. If he wouldn't listen, I'd deal with Leah myself. Because I wasn't "playing" detective.

I was following real clues.

And if someone didn't find the killer soon, how many more people might die?

∼

I strode out of the dining room, gestured to Alice, and headed over to the table in the lobby where Faye had provided muffins and egg-and-cheese biscuits for us to eat while we waited to be interviewed.

"Pretend you're hungry and have something more to eat," I whispered to Alice.

"That won't require any pretense. It's almost three o'clock in the afternoon, and all I've eaten since breakfast is one of these biscuits." Alice picked up a muffin and set it on a napkin. "What happened with Detective Harper?" She took a bite.

"He wouldn't listen to a word I said. As soon as he leaves, I want to talk to Leah again. Can you stick around for that?"

"Sure." Alice took another bite of her muffin, and I helped myself to one as well.

I only had one bite left when Detective Harper came out of the dining room. "We're done here," he said to Faye. He turned to the rest of the group. "You're free to go about your business, but don't leave town." He turned to talk to Officers Tate and Davis.

I angled my head toward the gift shop. Alice and I ducked inside and hid behind a display of local wines. With any luck, the detective would think we'd already left. I really didn't want another lecture.

The three police officers walked right past the gift shop without noticing us.

I ate the last of my muffin, wadded up my napkin, and, since I didn't see a trash can, shoved it into my big purse. "Let's see if we can catch Leah before she goes upstairs."

We stepped back into the lobby.

I quickly scanned it. Completely empty. "Drat. How did everyone—especially Leah—leave so fast? And how are we going to talk to her?"

Alice elbowed me.

Leah walked out of the dining room, stirring a large cup of coffee.

Alice and I hurried over.

"Leah, I'm so glad you're here. I wanted a chance to talk to you." I stuck my hands on my hips and spread my elbows wide, blocking as much of her path as possible.

"Oh?" Her face tightened.

My courage faltered. Did I really want to confront her head on? "Have, uh, have you heard anything yet about how Cordell is doing?"

"Only that they're taking him to Columbia." Her expression relaxed. "Heather is serving as the point person for the family. She's supposed to text us all if she learns anything."

"There are wonderful doctors in Columbia," I said. "Hopefully, Cordell will be fine." Enough wimpy small talk. Time to get some answers. "But I wonder if you really want Cordell to recover. After all, I saw you near the top of the stairs right after he fell."

Leah's eyes grew hard, and her backbone straightened. "My room is near the top of the stairs on the second floor. I certainly didn't push him down the stairs, if that's what you're insinuating."

I looked her in the eyes. "Then if I were you, I'd be careful. Brittany's been killed, and now there's been an attempt on Cordell's life. Personally, I'd be nervous that I might be the next family member attacked."

"Oh-hh." Alice's voice shifted higher. "I hadn't thought of that. I'd be nervous too."

"I'll be fine." Leah sniffed. "Brittany was never meant to die. Cordell was the intended victim all along."

I inhaled sharply. "How—how can you know that unless you're the killer?"

Leah rolled her eyes. "I am *not* the killer. I'm observant."

"What did you see?" Alice asked, her voice almost a whisper.

Leah looked at Alice, then at me. "That night at the museum, before Brittany collapsed, she muttered under her breath that the evening was going to be a royal pain to endure. She drank her wine, and when she realized that the woman who was refilling glasses was on the other side of the room, Brittany switched her empty glass with the full glass that Cordell had set by his plate."

My mouth fell open. "So the glass Brittany had in her hand when she died was—?"

"Cordell's."

Chapter Seventeen

I STARED AT LEAH. "Wow. So Brittany's death was an accident. The person who was supposed to die was Cordell."

The more I thought about it, the more I felt sick to my stomach. Murder was wrong, even if someone killed a woman who they'd known less than a year, a woman who was honestly rather despicable and stood between them and a huge sum of money. But in the back of my mind, I'd sort of hoped that Cordell had been mistaken when he said he was pushed down the stairs, or that someone had inadvertently bumped into him. Now, knowing what Leah had seen at the reception, it was clear that someone in the family had intended all along to murder Cordell, who was either their ex-husband, father, or grandfather.

"You see why I don't think I'm in any danger," Leah said.

"Have you told this to the police?" Alice asked.

Leah shook her head.

Seriously? I couldn't believe she'd kept such an important clue to herself. "Why not?"

Leah glanced at the floor. "Because, well, because I thought there was a chance—a tiny, tiny, tiny chance—that one of my boys might have killed Brittany." She covered her mouth with one hand for a second and looked away again. "I mean, I can't believe I'm even saying this, but Brad's business has been struggling lately, and Brittany was scheming to have Cordell change his will so that she would get all his money. Neither of my boys would have gotten a cent."

I didn't say a word. Every reply that came to mind called into question her character or that of her children.

Leah raised her chin. "I never should have doubted my son, and now I know that Brad is innocent because I saw him come out of the dining room after Cordell fell down the stairs. So he couldn't have been the person who pushed Cordell."

"You need to tell the police," I said.

"I know," Leah ran a hand down the leg of her dress pants. "I don't want anything to happen to Cordell. I tried to make myself tell the detective what I'd seen when I talked to him half an hour ago, but I chickened out. I'm afraid I'll get arrested for withholding evidence or something."

I bit my lip. Was that possible? I wasn't sure. She'd certainly made the investigation harder for the police, and for me. "I guess that's a chance you'll have to take if you want to be sure that whoever is trying to kill Cordell gets caught."

Leah let out an audible sigh. "You're right. I sort of

hoped everyone would get to go home and the killer would give up. I've tried to keep an eye on Cordell, but I couldn't protect him." She glanced at a clock on the lobby wall. "Do you think the detective in charge is already back in his office?"

"I bet he is." I'd also bet that he'd be pretty annoyed with her.

But at least we were closer to the truth. In less than a week in Dogwood Springs, there had been a murder and an attempted murder, and both times, the intended victim had been Cordell.

∽

The minute Alice and I were outside the B & B, I sent a text to the rest of our friends to tell them what we'd learned and invite them over to my apartment. Leah's information was big news that we needed to discuss.

While I was still holding my phone in my hand, it dinged with a text from Rodney.

Paula, who had been in custody, had been released. Her lawyer convinced the police that the evidence they had against her was circumstantial, that the murder of Brittany and the attempt on Cordell's life were connected, and that Paula couldn't have pushed Cordell down the stairs if she was locked up downtown.

Then replies to my invitation started coming in from my friends. Cleo had appointments until seven, so we agreed to meet shortly thereafter.

That gave me enough time to eat a quick dinner while watching "Antiques Roadshow," then put one of my dad's old Foreigner LPs on the turntable that had been his in college and tidy my apartment.

By seven fifteen the place was presentable, and soon Cleo, Zeke, Sam, Alice, Doug, and Bella were gathered in my living room.

Cleo's ankle was improving, but I brought over one of my dining chairs for her to prop her foot on.

"Thanks." She sank back into the couch, as if the day had taken all her energy.

"Are you sure you should be here, dear?" Alice looked at her. "We could fill you in tomorrow if you want to go upstairs and sleep."

"Nope. I just needed to sit down. And I made popcorn, but I didn't totally trust myself to carry it downstairs." She sent Zeke upstairs to get it, and I passed out small bowls and got everyone something to drink.

Once the popcorn had been passed around, Bella went from person to person, sniffing near their individual popcorn bowls.

"Remember what the vet said about people food, Bella." I got up, went to the kitchen, and came back with a dog biscuit.

After she was happily settled between me and Alice, gnawing away, I looked back at my friends. "Okay, guys, we need to regroup. Now that we know Cordell was the intended victim all along, it changes things.

Cleo tapped the table with one finger. "If we assume

that whoever killed Brittany was the same person who pushed Cordell down the stairs, then we know Brad wasn't the killer because you and Alice saw him on the first floor."

"And Paula couldn't have pushed Cordell," Alice said. "She was in jail."

"You know," Sam said. "We ruled out the mayor and the city council members as suspects in Brittany's murder because they didn't know her, but some of the people in local government must have known Cordell from when he grew up here."

"True." I thought for a moment. "But I really believe the murder and the attempted murder are connected, and the only people at the B & B besides Faye, the maid, Alice, and me, were four members of Cordell's family. I think our suspects are Heather and her son, Emmett, and Leah and her son, Nick. Let's go through each of them and think what motive they might have for killing Cordell."

"We should keep in mind that any one of them—or all of them—could have been lying earlier," Doug said.

He was right. Doug was a good addition to our group because he was naturally suspicious. Even if my gut said some of our suspects had been telling the truth when I spoke with them, I couldn't take those feelings as facts.

"As far as a motive for Heather," I said. "Let's say she lied, and she really was upset by Brittany's comments. She could be angry with Cordell because he didn't defend her. After all, he's her dad. Heather could think he should have loved her enough to protect her from Brittany's attacks."

"It doesn't seem to be the most likely scenario, at least not to me," Alice said.

"Emmett's still a good suspect," Doug said. "We only have his word that he was downstairs the whole time before Brittany was killed. With all that was going on, can you really be sure he didn't come upstairs at all?" He looked at Alice, then at me.

We exchanged glances, and both shook our heads. We'd been trying to run interference on family drama, watching for a spark of temper that might flare up and ruin the evening, not keeping track of the movements of every single person. "You know," I said, "when Emmett was downstairs, it would have given him plenty of time to find a place to later hide the poison vial."

"He's also the suspect who's a research chemist," Cleo said. "He'd know how to handle cyanide."

"Plus," Sam said. "If the initial theory was that Emmett killed Brittany to keep her from interfering with his inheritance, it also makes sense that he might have tried to kill Cordell at the museum before he could change his will. And he might have pushed Cordell down the stairs for the same reason—because he wanted money."

I scooped up a small handful of popcorn from my bowl. "I agree. Emmett is a strong suspect." I munched on my handful of popcorn and scooped up another bite.

"On the other hand," Zeke said, "we really don't know how much money the mysterious new backer of Nick's business was willing to contribute. And he could have bought some of the stuff that made the business look like it was expanding on credit, couldn't he?" Zeke glanced over at Sam.

"He sure could have. Good job thinking of things from a new angle." Sam beamed at Zeke like a proud older brother. "Nick might have killed Cordell either because he was angry that Cordell wouldn't fund his pottery gallery or—"

"Or because he wanted his inheritance immediately," I finished.

"Greed. Once again, a solid motive," Doug said as he reached toward the big popcorn bowl for a refill.

"I keep thinking about Leah." Cleo adjusted her foot on the chair. "We initially thought she killed Brittany because she was jealous after the divorce. Leah could just as easily have been angry with Cordell, angry enough to kill. When her first attempt failed and Brittany died, it could have been —for Leah—a happy coincidence."

"But she said she was afraid her son was the killer," Alice said. "And if she was the killer, why would she reveal that Cordell was the intended victim all along?"

"That could all be a giant ruse meant to throw people off," Cleo said.

"Wow." I refilled my popcorn bowl. "That would be really sneaky. I wouldn't put it past her, though." Motive and evidence aside, Leah struck me as the suspect who lied the easiest.

Zeke sat back in his chair. "So, if we take all that into account, it means we've got two suspects, Nick and Emmett, who might have killed because of greed." He held up two fingers. "Heather, who might have killed because she was hurt that her father didn't care how his new wife treated her." He added another finger.

"And Leah, who may have killed Cordell because she was angry that he divorced her," Cleo said.

Zeke held up a fourth finger.

"Four suspects," Alice said. "And we have no idea which one is guilty."

"Despite what Leah said, even if I wasn't Cordell, if I was a member of the Calhoun family, I'd be watching my back," Sam said. "I bet that each person's share of Cordell's money increases if one of the other heirs dies. So if Nick or Emmett tried to kill Cordell out of greed, they might be willing to kill someone else to increase their share of the inheritance."

"And the culprit already murdered Brittany," Doug added. "If someone has killed once, it's probably easier to kill again. The more they get away with, the bolder they might be."

I nodded slowly. "You're right. Somehow"—I looked around the room—"we've got to figure this out fast, before someone else gets killed."

Chapter Eighteen

THE NEXT DAY I had a long list of errands to run, including my regular Saturday trip to the grocery store and several other stops, like the bank and the drug store, most of which didn't welcome dogs. Normally, I tried to spend as much time as possible with Bella on the weekends, since she was home alone so much during the week, and I regretted leaving her home alone all morning.

To make matters worse, the whole time I was out running errands, my mind went over and over the suspects and the clues we had found.

Instead of figuring out who the killer was, all I accomplished was making myself nervous. The more I thought about the fact that the police hadn't found the poison vial when they searched the suspects, the more I worried that the vial might still be in the museum. And even though I didn't work on the weekends except for special events, Rodney and Imani each took a day, and volunteers were there, as well as guests. We had signs up asking visitors not to touch any of the displays, but some children—and some adults—ignored them. I imagined a child opening the vial of poison and shuddered.

Should I go over and check through all the displays?

No, the police had said the museum was safe.

I knew, though, now that I'd started worrying, I wouldn't trust their assessment until I checked the museum myself.

Once I got home, I called Sam. Would he be willing to meet me at the museum after dinner when it was closed and go through all the displays, just to reassure me that the vial of poison wasn't on the premises?

He would.

I let out a sigh of relief knowing I had a plan.

After lunch, I did a crossword puzzle and then, since the weather was still lovely, took Bella to the dog park. At first, she stayed close to me, more interested in attention than the open space. Eventually, when a couple of other dogs arrived with their owners, she ran off to play.

In the mud.

Luckily, I kept old towels in the back of my car for such emergencies. Once we got home, I gave her a bath. Just like every other time I'd bathed her, I got almost as wet as she did. But she looked so cute all covered in suds, and seemed so happy when I poured warm water over her, that I couldn't be mad when, despite my best efforts, she shook herself dry in the bathroom.

A good shake wasn't enough to dry her fur. She wasn't a

fan of the blow-dryer, but I toweled her off again and again. Finally, after dinner, when we needed to leave to meet Sam, her fur was mostly dry.

At ten after seven, I pulled into the parking lot behind the museum. Sam arrived a few moments later, and I hooked on Bella's leash and let her out.

"Hey, Sam," I called out, then hesitated. I appreciated that he'd been willing to come, but now that I'd gotten him here, I felt silly. "Thanks, uh, thanks for meeting me."

He walked over toward me. "No problem."

"I'm probably being paranoid. I mean, I really think that if there was cyanide in the building, the police would have found it. Otherwise, I wouldn't have brought Bella along. But I don't think I'll rest easy until I've gone through all the displays myself."

Sam bent down to pet Bella, and she gazed up at him with love. "I don't think you're being paranoid. I think you're a very responsible person, and you care about the museum, the people who work here, and the visitors. That responsibility and caring is part of what makes you special, Libby."

Tension eased in my chest, and I hugged him. "Thank you." I unlocked the back door and led the way in. After I told Bella to stay with me and behave, I let her off her leash. "No boot chewing," I warned her.

She rubbed her head against my leg and looked up at me with innocent eyes. Frankly, she seemed so starved for affection today that I doubted she would leave my side, except to be petted by Sam.

We started our search in the public space closest to the back door, the bathrooms. Sam took the men's room, and Bella and I checked the women's, but we found nothing. We moved on to a display about the first one-room schoolhouse in the town, back when it was called Silersville. I searched under old books, beneath the bench like the one the schoolchildren would have sat on, and through every drawer in the teacher's desk. Sam peered deep inside a wood stove we'd found from the period, a piece similar to one that would have been the sole source of heat for the schoolhouse.

Suddenly, Bella barked from the other room.

"Bella, what's going on? You were supposed to stay with me." I walked through the doorway and flipped on the lights, illuminating the display where she'd found the boot, an exhibit set up to look like a bedroom in the 1890s.

Everything looked normal, except that, although I wasn't sure when he'd managed it, Rodney had rearranged the display. That was so like Rodney. He'd assured me there hadn't been any damage but had taken time to make the boots less visible because he knew I was uncomfortable with what Bella had done. He'd even added a couple of new artifacts and redone a placard that a young guest had damaged.

Bella continued barking, her body rigid, her nose pointed at the top of a dresser.

"Hush, girl." I patted her shoulder and looked over at Sam. "You'd think there was a squirrel in here."

"It could be a mouse." Sam stepped closer to the dresser.

"I hope not." I'd hate to think that a mouse may have been destroying some of the museum's documents or historic clothing.

Sam pulled his phone out of his pocket and turned on the flashlight. "Bella seems focused on things on top of the dresser." He pointed. "What's this, some kind of fancy covered soup bowl?"

I couldn't help but giggle. The small porcelain dish was about the size of a soup bowl, except it had a lid with a hole in the top large enough for a woman to fit a couple of her fingers through. "Hardly. That's a porcelain hair receiver made in the early 1900s, possibly the very late 1800s. It's a nice example with a clear manufacturer's mark on the base."

"What did you say it is?"

"A hair receiver. A woman would have saved hair in there after she cleaned out her hairbrush so that it could be used to fill a ratt."

"A rat?"

"Ratt with two T's. That was a homemade hairpiece. Women used them to puff out those big hairstyles in Victorian times."

Sam shook his head. "You do know the most unusual things, Libby."

I grinned. "All part of the job."

He shone the flashlight down the hole at the top of the hair receiver. "There's something in here." He angled the light. His eyebrows rose, and he handed me his phone. "Don't touch, but take a look."

I pointed the light into the hair receiver.

Inside sat a small glass vial containing a bit of white powder, powder that was probably cyanide.

∾

"Come on, girl, let's get you out of this room." I pulled Bella back from the dresser. "We'd better call Detective Harper."

I turned to Sam, but he was already dialing as I led Bella to the front hall.

She came willingly, without a single bark, and showed no interest in anything else in the room, not even the boot she'd chewed on earlier in the week. Had all that barking been to lead us to the poison vial?

After about ten minutes, Detective Harper arrived, and we showed him what we'd found.

He took several photos, then put on gloves and removed the vial from the hair receiver. "I'm not going to open it and smell it, but I'd say this is the murder weapon. The team's going to get an earful for missing this, I'll tell you." He slid the vial into a plastic evidence bag. "How did you find it?"

I explained what Bella had done.

He paused and looked at her for a long moment. "I know some dogs can be trained to sniff out poison, but Don never mentioned that Bella had been through any type of training. He just said she was the smartest dog in town."

Don Felding, who had been Bella's owner and the former resident of my apartment until he passed away, had been a retired FBI agent. On previous occasions, Bella had shown herself to be quite the canine detective, seriously impressing Detective Harper. He might not always be eager to hear my theories on murder suspects, but he always respected Bella's input.

Sam turned to me. "You said Bella was in this room recently, didn't you, Libby?"

"Yes, this is where she got in trouble for chewing on that boot." I pointed, then shot an embarrassed glance at the detective. "She slipped away when I had her in my office upstairs one evening."

"I guess there's a chance," Sam said, "that Bella didn't know what she smelled was poison, simply that it was a very different smell from what was here the other day."

Detective Harper took off his gloves and ran a hand over his chin. "We checked the whole museum. You would think there'd be all sorts of new smells." He gazed at Bella again. "You really are smart." He bent down, patted her back, and told her what a good dog she was.

After a moment he stood up. "Libby, I must apologize for telling you the museum was safe before. And I'll need to have the team go over this room again. The museum can stay open, but this room will have to be off-limits."

Once word got out that the museum had been open while there was a bottle of poison in one of the displays, it wouldn't matter whether the museum doors were open or not. We weren't going to have any visitors. And I could only imagine the reaction of the volunteer who hadn't wanted to work her shift in the gift shop today. I'd thought she was being paranoid, but she'd been completely correct.

The detective pulled a pen from his jacket pocket and labeled the plastic evidence bag. "Can you meet me here at eight tomorrow morning so the team can get started? I expect the killer wore gloves while handling the vial, but we might get lucky and find that they left some trace evidence like a strand of hair in that ceramic dish thing."

"Yes, I'll be here." I thought of telling him how ironic it would be if the police found a strand of hair, since the ceramic "dish thing" was actually a Victorian hair receiver, but it didn't seem to matter. All that mattered was that while I was director, the museum had been open for three days with actual poison on display. It was only through sheer luck that no one had died.

"I'll need a list of everyone who has been here the past three days so we can contact them to make sure no one was harmed," the detective added.

"I'll get that right now," I said.

The list, thankfully, was short. Imani, Rodney, and myself, three volunteers, and eight names that I copied down from the guest book—one of them Dallas, Sam's boss's wife. My stomach churned at the thought of something happening to her. Then I glanced back down at the guest book and spotted a name higher up on the page that made me stop.

Leah Calhoun. And two names above her name was her son's, Nick Calhoun.

"Look," I showed the names to Detective Harper. "Both Leah and Nick were in the museum on Thursday. Wouldn't you think if one of them was the killer, and they'd hidden the vial, that they would retrieve it?"

"Probably," the detective said. "Although, if they wore gloves, they might have thought they wouldn't have left any evidence."

I thought about what he said. "But if I was the killer, I'd be worried that I might have touched the vial without wearing gloves before I put the cyanide in it. The vial doesn't have a label, so it must not have been sold with the cyanide in it." My words tumbled out as it all came together in my mind. "And since I already narrowed the suspect list down to Leah, Nick, Emmett, and Heather, if we rule out Nick and Leah, the most likely suspect is Emmett or Heather."

Detective Harper's nostrils flared. "Libby, didn't I tell you only yesterday that you shouldn't have a suspect list? You need to stay out of this."

"Really?" I planted my hands on my hips and looked at him in disbelief. "If I'd stayed out of this, some child might have found the poison vial when they visited the museum with a school group."

Sam stepped closer, to stand beside me. "She's got a point, detective."

"Incompetent idiots, missing something practically in plain sight," the detective muttered. "Okay. I give up. I can't keep you from trying to find the killer. But at least try to be careful." He turned on his heel and strode out of the building.

"Thanks, Sam." I rested a hand on his arm. "For backing me up and for being here with me. This situation is a mess."

"It is, and the police aren't doing a very good job, but I do agree with the detective on one thing." Sam looked over at me. "You need to be careful."

I nodded, and then I sent a text to Imani, Rodney, and all the board members, letting them know the situation. I made the executive decision that the museum would be closed on Sunday. It was far easier to have a sign on the door than to explain to any visitors that one room was off-limits because poison had been found there the day before, when the museum had been open.

Sam and I said goodnight, and Bella and I went home. I tried to go to bed early, but tossed and turned all night, thinking about how museum guests might have been injured. Or worse.

When I woke, it was bright and sunny, and I slowly realized that the sound I heard was not my alarm, which I'd forgotten to set, but a phone call.

I grabbed my phone from the nightstand and mumbled a sleepy hello to Faye.

"Libby? I've got big news about the murder." Faye's words came out a mile a minute.

"What?"

"About ten minutes ago, I went into clean Emmett's room. You'll never believe what I found."

Chapter Nineteen

"WHAT DID YOU FIND?" Really, I wasn't awake enough to play guessing games with Faye.

"Emmett had a bottle labeled sodium cyanide sitting right on the desk in his room."

I sat bolt upright in bed. "Sodium cyanide?"

"When I read the label, I almost had a heart attack."

"So what did you do?" I put the phone on speaker and got out of bed.

"I took a photo of the bottle on the desk, tried to make the room look like I hadn't been in there yet, and then I ran downstairs and checked on my phone to be sure. I learned that sodium cyanide is one form of the poison. Then I called the police."

"Taking a photo was really smart," I said. "That way even if Emmett comes back and hides the cyanide, you have proof."

"Thanks," Faye said. "I think Emmett is out for a run, but as soon as he returns, I bet he'll be arrested."

I asked Faye to keep me updated, hung up, and got in the shower.

Half an hour later, Bella and I went upstairs so I could tell Cleo what had happened. She and Zeke were sitting in her kitchen, eating toaster waffles.

"Hey, Libby," Zeke snuck Bella a piece of bacon that he thought I didn't see, then stabbed a bite of waffle with his fork. "Mom sent me over to borrow Cleo's glue gun for some craft project she's doing, and I arrived just in time for breakfast."

"Your second breakfast." Cleo laughed. "Want some waffles, Libby?"

My stomach rumbled. Breakfast smelled wonderful. "Sure." I'd been so excited about Faye's news that I'd forgotten to eat.

Cleo started to get up, but I waved her back to her seat, got two waffles out of a family pack I found in the freezer, and popped them in the toaster while I explained what Faye had found.

Zeke let out a low whistle. "It does make sense. As a chemist, Emmett would be more comfortable handling poison than most people."

Cleo nodded. "Plus, when he was downstairs during the reception, he could have been scoping out a place to hide the poison bottle. We only have his word that he didn't come upstairs." She tipped her head to one side. "I wonder, if you knew what you were doing, how long would it take to slip upstairs and pour poison in Cordell's wine glass?"

"I wouldn't think it would take very long," I said as I sat down with my waffles. "We had place cards on the table showing where everyone would sit, and it wouldn't be much harder than putting sugar in a glass. With Faye finding the poison bottle in Emmett's room at the B & B, it's almost like finding a smoking gun." I added two strips of bacon to my plate and shook my head at Zeke as he attempted to give Bella another piece. "But if Emmett had the brains to hide the poison vial, why would he leave the bottle of cyanide out in the open in his room? He has to realize housekeeping comes in the rooms."

"You never know," Cleo said. "Even if he's smart, he has to mess up sometime."

"Maybe, but the more I think about it, the less I believe it. It's too easy." I buttered my waffles and topped them with a generous swirl of maple syrup. "I wish I could talk to him."

"The police are probably already at the B & B," Cleo said. "But if not, and if Emmett is the killer, you'd be putting yourself in a lot of danger." She tipped her head to one side. "I know, I know. I'm not usually the cautious one, but confronting him again seems risky."

"True." I dragged a bite of waffle through the syrup on my plate and tried to tell myself the case was solved.

By the time Cleo and I had finished our waffles and Zeke had eaten another stack of four, I still wasn't convinced. "What if I call Paula and casually ask how things are going? If Emmett's already been arrested, she'd probably know."

"It couldn't hurt." Cleo cleared our plates and wiped some goo from the bottom of the syrup bottle off the table.

I dialed, and Paula answered on the first ring.

"Oh, Libby, I'm so glad you called. When I wanted the police to consider someone else besides me as the murderer, I never wanted them to arrest my grandson." She launched into a rather long story about what a sweet little boy Emmett had been.

I expressed my sympathies.

"You've got to help him, Libby," Paula said.

"I admit, I have my doubts, but I'm not really sure what to do at this point."

"If only you could find that girl who works for the caterers," Paula said. "She's his alibi."

"Hold on." I explained who I was with and put the phone on speaker. "You were saying that Emmett has someone who can give him an alibi?"

"He does!" Even over the phone, I could hear how desperate Paula sounded. "He couldn't have possibly put the poison in the wine that Brittany drank because he was downstairs the whole time."

"He did tell me he was looking at displays on the first floor," I said.

"We-ell," Paula said. "That wasn't exactly true. He was actually talking with a girl who worked for the caterers. He didn't want to get the girl in trouble with her boss. She was working the event alone while her boss ran back to their commercial kitchen to get something they forgot. But instead of checking on the food, she and Emmett were talking."

Hmmm. The only girl I'd seen that night had looked a lot younger than Emmett, too young to be someone he should have been chatting up. On the other hand, if his story was true, it might explain why we ran out of chicken tenders. And, although I wasn't sure how someone else would have gotten a key to Emmett's room at the B & B, that cyanide bottle might have been planted and—

"But the police can't seem to find this girl," Paula wailed.

"What's her name?" Zeke asked.

"Emmett doesn't know her last name, but her first name is Destiny," Paula said. "She has long, blond hair with a pink streak."

"Oh-hh," Cleo said. "Destinee, with two Es at the end. Destinee Brown."

"The police apparently figured out who she was," Paula said. "But she's not answering her phone, and no one is home at her parent's house."

Zeke leaned over on the couch and muttered something under his breath to Cleo that I couldn't hear.

"Paula, this is Cleo. Give us a little while. I think we may be able to find Destinee."

"Really?" Paula's voice rose. "Oh, my goodness, that would be amazing."

A zing of excitement ran through me. Even on a case like this, when all the suspects were from out of town, my friends' small-town connections were proving useful. I said goodbye to Paula, hung up, and looked at Cleo and Zeke. "Well?"

"I know Destinee." Zeke wadded up his napkin and tossed it on the table. "She's not the brightest in math, so we're in the same class, even though she's a senior and I'm a sophomore. I didn't mean to be eavesdropping, but I heard her and her friends talking on Friday."

I was right. The girl was still in high school, and Emmett was what? Twenty-five? But that didn't make Emmett a murderer. I gestured for Zeke to keep going.

"Destinee's parents are in Jamaica for two weeks. Her mom won a trip because she sold a bunch of candles or something. They left Destinee at home alone." Zeke cocked his head to one side. "Talk about a bad idea."

"She's just like her cousins, who I went to school with," Cleo said. "Party, party, party."

"But the police aren't going to find her with her phone because Destinee is grounded, and her parents turned off her phone and took it with them. Like she's going to stay home with them out of town..." Zeke covered his mouth with his fist and silently chuckled. "Destinee and her two best friends and their boyfriends all planned to spend the whole weekend at her parents' cabin on the Gasconade River."

"That's about half an hour from here," Cleo explained to me.

I thought for a moment. If Detective Harper had arrested Emmett and thought he was the killer, he'd probably remove the police protection from Cordell, leaving him vulnerable to attack from the real killer. The most important thing was to convince the detective that Emmett was innocent as quickly as possible. "Did Destinee say where on the river the cabin is, Zeke? If we told Detective Harper, he could drive out and get a statement."

"No idea," Zeke said.

"I know where that cabin is," Cleo said. "I went there once with Destinee's cousins."

I looked over at her.

"Not for one of their drunken weekends. After a float trip. I don't know the address, but I could find it."

I stood up. "What are we waiting for?"

~

By three o'clock, Cleo and I were nearing the Gasconade River.

Zeke was home, having promised his mom he'd help with yard work.

Instead, Cleo and I had brought Bella, who always helped me make friends.

The day was so warm, close to sixty, that it was hard to believe only a few days earlier, the night of the reception, we'd had a few flakes of snow. This early in the spring, most of the trees were still gray and leafless, but every now and then, I got a good view of the river, which was wide and smooth. I could envision the banks lined with green trees in the summer. A cabin looking out over the scene would be idyllic.

Some of the landmarks that Cleo remembered, like a billboard for an annual fish fry, were gone, and we made several wrong turns on gravel roads. But after we went around an especially tight curve, Cleo pointed ahead.

"Another mile or two," she said. "We're close."

We passed a driveway that Cleo peered at, then shook her head and drove on. "There it is." She pointed and parked her Jeep behind a shiny, red pickup truck.

The cabin was much nicer than many we had passed and far bigger than I'd expected. Two stories, with cedar siding stained a dark green, it reminded me of fancy lake houses I'd seen. "Destinee's mother sells candles. What does her dad do?"

"Not a lot," Cleo said. "Family money."

We got out, and I put Bella on her leash. The three of us climbed the wide, wooden steps to a deep front porch.

Cleo knocked on the door.

There was a shriek from inside, a rustling sound, and then silence.

Bella quirked her head to one side, and Cleo knocked again.

The blinds of a window on the front of the house cracked open, and a few seconds later, the girl who'd brought the chicken tenders up to the reception at the museum opened the door.

The night of the reception, her hair had been up in a bun,

and her makeup had been a bit overdone, but attractive. Today her hair was pulled back in a messy ponytail, her mascara was flaking off, and her face was sweaty and blotchy.

Behind her, two other girls peered out at us, both similarly disheveled.

Destinee blinked as if the bright sunlight was painful. "Cleo? What are you doing here?

"Hey, Destinee, this is my friend, Libby. We need to talk to you."

Destinee scrunched up her face and looked at me. "You're the lady from the museum, right? More chicken tenders?"

"Yes, I'm Libby Ballard, the museum director." I patted Bella. "And this is Bella. Are you okay with dogs?"

Destinee looked down and immediately knelt to pet Bella.

Bella licked her cheek.

Destinee giggled and stood. "Very okay. Uh, come in." She gestured us in, and glanced around, wincing. "My girlfriends and I are ... cleaning up. Things got a bit wild here over the weekend." She placed a hand on Cleo's arm. "Please, don't tell my mom. She'd kill me for letting the place get this bad."

Cleo and I stepped inside and sat on matching green plaid chairs in what before the weekend had probably been a beautiful, casual living room. Currently, it resembled the remains of a tornado with the addition of empty beer cans on tabletops and the faint smell of weed and vomit in the air. Hopefully, this conversation wouldn't take long. I was already longing to be back outside.

Bella happily wandered off with the other two girls, who both exclaimed about how sweet she was. Despite what they'd done to the house, these girls couldn't be all bad if Bella liked them.

"We're here about Emmett Ford," I said. "I think you met him the night you worked the reception at the museum."

"Yeah. I remember him." Destinee's mouth twisted up.

"He's a chief suspect in the death of the woman who was poisoned upstairs," I said. "The police have been trying to reach you to see if you can provide him with an alibi."

"My parents took my phone. I won't get it back until Wednesday, when they get home." She muttered something under her breath about how unfair the punishment was. "Emmett was downstairs the whole time until we heard people screaming upstairs. So I can provide him with an alibi, but I don't necessarily want to." Destinee crossed her arms over her chest. "He was a creep. I told him I wasn't interested in seeing him, but he kept hitting on me, and he wouldn't leave me alone. So if he rots in prison, it's fine with me."

Heat built in my chest. "He didn't do anything to you other than talk, did he?"

Gratitude flashed through Destinee's eyes. "No, he was just a pest."

Cleo leaned in. "I understand how you feel, Destinee, but if the police think Emmett was the killer, they aren't trying to find the real killer. And the real killer could try again to kill Cordell Calhoun, and this time they might succeed."

Destinee's eyes grew wide. "Oh, I didn't think of that. My boyfriend will be really peeved if I'm responsible for that old guy dying before he makes his big donation to the high school football program."

I made a face. Not the nicest reason to do her civic duty and tell the police the truth, but it would work. "So you'll talk to Detective Harper?"

"We've got another two hours of cleaning here at least before I can drive home." She looked around and shuddered. "Probably more. But I'll borrow a phone from one of my friends and call him. If he wants, once I'm back in Dogwood Springs, I'll stop by the police station."

"Thank you." Cleo stood. "I'm sorry Emmett was a jerk, but you're doing the right thing." She moved toward the door.

I called Bella and, after one last pat from each of the girls, she joined me. "None of my business," I said as I left, "but you might want to open a window or two."

Destinee nodded. "Good idea."

Cleo, Bella, and I escaped outside, and I inhaled deeply. "Finally, fresh air."

"If she gets that place clean enough to please her mom, it will surprise me," Cleo said.

"Me too." I let Bella in the back seat and climbed in the Jeep. "But I'm glad we found her. If Emmett's not the killer, we know it has to be Heather."

"Maybe the poison bottle was in Emmett's room because he found out what his mom had done and took the poison from her because he knew how to safely dispose of it," Cleo said.

"I bet you're right. The only problem is that we've come to the conclusion that Heather is the killer because we ruled everyone else out. We don't have any real proof that she committed the crime. How are we going to convince Detective Harper?"

Cleo started the engine. "I have no idea."

"Let's think about this," I said.

By the time we were back on Elm Street, we had a plan. I wasn't sure it would be successful, and it certainly wouldn't be pleasant, but we had to try something if we were going to stop Heather.

Chapter Twenty

"THAT'S WHAT I SMELL—SOUR milk," Cleo whispered and pointed to a clump of soggy cereal and wet paper napkins near the edge of the plastic tarp. "Pee-uu." She fanned one hand in front of her face and backed closer to the gate of the fenced area that hid the trashcans from view at the Hilltop B & B.

Bella nosed in and licked up a piece of the soggy cereal.

"Bella, no!" I scolded in a low voice, then pushed her back and told her to sit.

Would sour milk make her sick? Hopefully not. When I envisioned going through the trash from the bed-and-breakfast to search for clues, I'd been so focused on trying to prove that Heather was the murderer that I'd forgotten where some of the trash would come from. The first bag had been no problem. It was from the guestrooms. But the second bag and this third bag were clearly from the kitchen. As soon as I dumped out the second bag of trash, Bella wanted to roll in it. I managed to prevent that, but in addition to that bite of cereal, she'd managed to gobble down a sausage patty. At least the sausage looked fresh.

"I don't know if going through this trash was a good idea," Cleo said. "We haven't found a single clue that links Heather to the murder."

"I know." I looked at the two big, rolling trash cans and let out a dejected sigh. "It was kind of a long shot, but it was the best idea I had."

"I still think we should have disguised ourselves as maids and snooped in the guest rooms," Cleo said.

"Faye has worked so hard to build the reputation of the B & B. She'd never let us violate her guests' privacy like that." I gestured to the trash I'd spread out on the tarp. "This is all from the kitchen, so there's no reason to pick through it piece by piece. And the less time the food scraps are available to Bella, the better." I quickly rolled up the tarp. Cleo held the trash bag open, and I picked up the tarp and shook the trash back into the bag.

Or at least most of it.

Three banana peels landed on the concrete. Half an eggshell bounced off my shoe and joined them, leaving a clear, sticky trail from the shell to my shoelace.

Bella licked my shoe.

I picked up the banana peels and eggshell and added them to the trash bag, grateful I was wearing thick rubber gloves.

Cleo reknotted the bag and moved it to one side, then

adjusted her gloves and picked up her flashlight, which was becoming more necessary with every passing minute.

"I'm going to have to wash my entire outfit with disinfectant, including my shoes," I said as I studied a drain near the back of the fence. "And tomorrow I'll have to come back here and hose down this area, so Faye doesn't have to."

The trash area wasn't visible from the B & B, hidden by the wooden fence and the branches of an oak tree overhead, but it was just off the corner of the building. If I left a rotting mess out here, anyone going around the building from the parking lot to the back yard would smell it.

An hour ago, when Cleo and I had been driving back from talking to Destinee at the river, I'd hoped we'd find a clue in the trash from the guest rooms that would link Heather to the murder, like a receipt for when she bought the cyanide.

Clearly, I'd been overly optimistic. So far, all we'd found was a mountain of dirty tissues and proof that one of the Calhouns was very fond of Cheetos. Despite the thick rubber gloves I was wearing, I felt like I needed an hour-long shower. And now the sun had dipped below the treetops. We were losing light. Soon we'd be out here in complete darkness, and the beam from Cleo's flashlight would be noticeable, even with the fence and the branches from the oak.

"Maybe there was a clue, but it got picked up by the garbage collectors," I said. "Faye did say this is only the trash from yesterday and today."

"Maybe you're right," Cleo agreed.

"There's only one more bag to go through." I spread the plastic tarp back out on the concrete and emptied the last trash bag.

It was full of tissues and wadded-up papers, not kitchen trash. One by one, I uncrumpled the wadded-up papers, held them up to the beam from Cleo's flashlight, and tried to identify them, hoping I'd find some mention of cyanide. Instead, I found gas receipts, fast-food receipts, three separate copies of the program from the mayor's reception, and some heavy art paper with sketches of vases and pitchers, which I assumed were ideas Nick had rejected.

One wad of paper was compressed into an almost perfect ball. It rolled off the tarp and into the corner of the trash area.

Bella nudged it back toward me with her nose.

Better to keep her occupied with a ball, even if it was paper, than to have her licking up rotten egg white from the concrete. I batted the paper ball back to her and opened a crumpled fast-food bag. I found exactly what you'd expect—six stale French fries, a bit of uneaten bun, and a blob of ketchup squished all over the wax paper wrapper that had once held a burger.

"Nothing." I threw down the fast-food bag and folded the plastic tarp around the trash.

Bella nudged her ball of paper back to me, and I gave it a gentle kick, sending it back into the corner for her to chase.

Then I funneled the tarp into the trash bag, and, since all the tissues were now stuck to the residue from kitchen trash, shoved the tarp into the bag with the trash. "What a waste of time. But at least we're done and can go home. I'm getting cold." I'd worn several layers, topped by a sweatshirt, instead of my coat because I didn't want to get garbage on it.

The big HVAC unit behind the trash area kicked on as if to confirm that the temperature drop wasn't my imagination, and Bella nudged her paper ball back to me.

"One last piece of trash, huh, girl?" I picked up the paper. I'd pretty much given up on finding a clue but, acting on autopilot after unfolding all those other wadded-up papers, I uncrumpled it.

My mind somersaulted as I stared at the thick paper. Facts that hadn't seemed important at the time tumbled into place, and my mouth went dry. "Cleo, look."

She shone the light more closely on the paper. "Is it a receipt for the cyanide? Or some kind of packing slip?"

"No, but it makes it really clear who the killer is, and it's not Heather." I held the paper toward her and pointed to a drawing, marked through with a heavy scribble made in anger—or in anguish. Under the scribble, drawn at about four times normal size, was a sketch of a ring with a large center stone. Curved around it, were the letters B and N.

"A ring?" Cleo sounded confused.

I nodded. It all made sense now. "The killer is Nick. He drew this because—"

Cleo turned off her flashlight. "Shhh," she whispered. "I think I saw a light."

My muscles tensed, and I looked from side to side, but I saw nothing.

Nothing ... until the gate to the trash area burst open.

Nick stood in the doorway, using his phone as a flashlight and pointing a gun at Cleo.

Bella let out a low growl.

My stomach knotted, and my heart rate sped. "Steady, Bella." I rested a hand on her back. I didn't want Nick shooting anyone—not Cleo or Bella or me.

Nick turned off the light on his phone, slid it into the pocket of his jeans, and ripped the paper away from me. "I'll take that," he said with a sneer. "I knew when I saw your car in the parking lot that you were sticking your nose in where it didn't belong. And don't bother screaming. Thanks to that HVAC unit, no one can hear you."

~

Cleo's eyes swirled with fear and confusion, and then the self-defense training she'd had in New York must have kicked in.

Her jaw set. Her eyes flickered to Nick's feet, then to the small plastic flashlight she held, then to the gun in his hand.

The knot in my stomach grew even tighter. It had been five years since Cleo lived in New York. Were her skills sharp enough to disable Nick and not get herself killed in the process? She might stand a chance if she had a large, heavy, metal flashlight, but with that little thing? I didn't know much about self-defense, only what I'd read once in a magazine at the dentist's office, but disarming a large guy like Nick couldn't be easy. From what that article said, we'd be better off running or talking to Nick, trying to convince him not to kill us.

I shook my head at Cleo. It was too big a risk to take. I couldn't bear it if she risked her life to save mine.

Plus, if we kept Nick talking, there was a chance someone might come outside and overhear him. At the very least, if we stalled, it would get darker, which might give Cleo and me a better chance of escape.

I looked at Nick. "How are you handling it, knowing that you killed the woman you loved?" I asked softly. "Did it start at some family function? Christmas, maybe?"

He stared at me for a long moment and then shrugged. "Yeah, it began at Christmas. I guess it doesn't matter if I admit it. You won't be telling anyone else once I force you out into the woods and shoot you."

Force us into the woods and shoot us? I gulped.

Cleo's eyes grew wide. "You had an affair with your stepmom?"

"It's not like it sounds," he said quickly. "She was my age, not the age of a stepmom. And at first, I was simply trying to be decent to her, not hateful like Paula and Heather were to my mom when I was little." His lips stretched into a rueful smile. "Once we started talking, though, Brittany and I sort of clicked."

I nodded. "And because you both lived in Nashville, you were able to keep seeing each other."

He glanced away, then looked back at me. "Early on, I tried to break it off. But she ... well, I think she loved the forbidden aspect of our relationship. It made it more exciting. And after a while, I couldn't imagine my life without her."

Hmmm. Nick's emotions may have been genuine, but it didn't sound to me like Brittany had loved Cordell or Nick.

Cleo's forehead bunched up. "But how did you manage to see each other without Cordell finding out?"

"She put me in her phone as Nikki, and said if Dad ever asked, she'd say I was a girlfriend. We communicated as little as possible, using code words for the places we met. 'The gym' was my apartment. 'A pedicure' was a meal in a place outside Nashville that no one in our crowd would ever visit."

"It wasn't enough, though, was it?" I said. "If your dad was dead, you could have your inheritance and have Brittany all to yourself."

A flicker of guilt passed through his eyes, then they hardened. "He'd had a good life. And every time Brittany and I said goodbye, she hated leaving, hated going back to their house."

"Couldn't she have gotten a divorce?" Cleo asked.

Yeah. Good question. I exchanged glances with her.

Nick's mouth twisted to one side. "He'd have left Brittany with nothing. After Mom, he said he was never getting married without an ironclad prenup."

I winced. How could Nick not have realized that if Brittany wouldn't leave Cordell without his money, she didn't really love him? What a fool.

But that fool, of course, was the one with the gun. "But how did she end up dead? Didn't she know where you were putting the poison?"

"She didn't even know I was using poison. She said I shouldn't tell her how I planned to kill him because she was too sensitive to handle it if she knew."

Sensitive? Plausible deniability was more like it. If everything went sideways, Brittany didn't want to go to jail.

"Brittany"—his voice cracked—"Brittany trusted me." Nick shook his head rapidly from side to side, as if driving out the memory. "Enough of this." He repositioned the gun in front of him and used it to gesture to the gate. "Head toward the woods."

My lungs went rigid, barely able to let air in or out. No one had come outside. No one knew what was happening.

Bella must have sensed my tension. She growled again, but I patted her back and managed to calm her. If I could just stall a little longer, it would be pitch black, and we might have a better chance of escape.

"Wait, tell me one more thing," I cried. "How did you hide the cyanide vial?"

Nick's forehead crinkled. "I thought you knew that too."

"No, I don't."

"After I slipped the poison into Dad's wine glass, I kept the vial in my jacket pocket and made some excuse about using the restroom. Then I sneaked downstairs and dropped the vial in that flowered dish."

"The hair receiver," I corrected, unable to stop myself.

"The what?"

"The hair receiver," I said. "Back in Victorian times, women saved hair from their hairbrushes. They'd use it to fill a homemade hairpiece. Or make art," I quickly added.

"Art?" He sounded interested.

If we got out of this alive, it was because I knew my audience. I could easily talk about Victorian art until night had completely fallen. "A woman would gather a bunch of hair about the size of a pencil lead, brush it smooth, and then twist it until it curled over on itself into loops. She'd pin the loops to fabric and make flowers out of them, with each loop as a petal. Often, it was part of the grieving process, a way to remember someone who had died by using their hair. In a time when they didn't have photography, anything that could help them remember their loved one was precious."

"Weird," he said, "but I guess they used what they had."

"Exactly." I was about to launch into a talk I'd once given about Victorian-era crafts when Nick raised the gun again. Apparently, his interest in art was not as strong as his interest in killing us. I changed the subject and talked faster. "So why didn't you retrieve the vial that day you came to the museum?"

"Because every time I tried to go into the room with the vial, that old fart was fussing around with the display. I hung around as long as I could, but with a dinky little museum like yours, it's only believable for someone to stay for so long."

My chest grew hot. How dare he call Rodney an "old fart" or the Dogwood Springs History Museum "dinky"?

Forget about trying to escape in the dark. I had a better idea.

I drew in a deep breath, gathered my strength, and shoved one of the big rolling trash cans at Nick.

He stumbled backward and fell to the ground with an *oomph*.

Adrenaline poured into my veins, and I opened the gate wide. "Run," I yelled to Cleo and Bella.

I pushed Cleo out ahead of me, and the three of us raced toward the back door of the B & B.

Chapter Twenty-One

LESS THAN A MINUTE LATER, Cleo, Bella, and I burst into the lobby of the bed-and-breakfast.

"Please, get Bella somewhere safe," I gasped to Cleo. "And call the cops. I've got a plan, but we'll need backup."

She nodded and slipped a hand through Bella's collar to hurry her toward the dining room.

Then I started up the stairs toward the second floor. "Fire!" I shouted. "Fire! Use the stairs!"

I'd barely gotten the words out when Nick thundered into the lobby.

I hunched down and peered over the side of the stairs.

He had turned away, searching for me, and didn't see me.

As quietly as I could, I started climbing the stairs.

But then I heard footsteps move farther into the lobby. "Gotcha."

My throat tightened, and I turned around.

Nick stood at the bottom of the stairs, pointing the gun right at me.

My heart pounded so hard that it felt like it might burst out of my chest.

I had thought my plan would work.

I had thought I could stop him.

I had thought someone would hear me.

But instead, he had me in his sights, and—

"Where's the fire?" Brad appeared at the top of the stairs with his hair lopsided, as if he'd been lying in bed watching TV. Leah rushed out to join him, wearing one strappy sandal and holding the other one, which she quickly slipped on.

My breath whooshed out. They *had* heard me.

"There's no fire," I told them, and I turned to face Nick. "But you're not really going to shoot me in front of your own mother, are you?"

His eyes grew hard, his jaw tensed, and he glared at me, but the hand with the gun shook.

And then, from behind me, Leah let out a high-pitched wail.

She ran down the stairs past me, toward Nick. "Oh, honey, no," she cried. "Whatever's going on, you've got to stop. Killing Libby will only make it worse."

"Mom!" he shouted, sounding like a petulant teenager. His face tightened, and he looked at her, then at me, then back at her.

His lower lip quivered, and he slowly lowered the gun to his side.

"Now, give me that." Leah held out her hand.

Nick's face crumpled, and, after a long moment, he gave her the weapon.

And Officers Tate and Davis burst into the lobby.

∽

Ten minutes later, Detective Harper arrived. Once he checked that the officers had things under control, he strode over toward where Cleo, Bella, and I sat on one of the big tan couches. His dark eyebrows were bunched up, and his lips were narrowed to a tight line.

"Libby," he said sharply. "I thought I told you to stay out of this case."

"If I had, would it have gotten solved?" I shot him an incredulous look. "Honestly, did you suspect Nick?"

He flushed. "Sort of."

Yeah, right. Nick wouldn't have been stopped without me, my friends, and—most of all—the smartest dog in town.

As if Bella wanted to show she was a good sport in any competition, she walked over to the detective and leaned her head against his leg.

He patted her and glanced over at me. "I know Bella found the murder weapon, but did she also help you figure out the killer?"

"She's the one who found the drawing that pulled it all together when we went through the trash."

His eyes narrowed. "The drawing that proved that Nick and Brittany were an item," he said under his breath.

Bella nudged his leg, and he sat down on the couch facing me.

I explained all I knew about the murder and the attempted murder, as well as how Bella had rolled the wadded-up drawing to me again and again.

He rubbed between Bella's ears. "Were you just interested in that paper because it was scrunched up into a ball, girl, or are you smarter than both Libby and me put together?"

Bella wagged her tail and gave us both a doggy grin.

I looked at Detective Harper. "I guess we'll never know, but she sure seems good at finding clues, doesn't she?"

"She sure does," he agreed.

~

The next evening, I invited my friends over to my house after dinner to celebrate the fact that the killer was behind bars—and that Cleo, Bella, and I were still alive.

"Alice and Doug are here." Sam pointed out my living room window.

"Wonderful." I finished setting forks and napkins on the table. "Alice said she was running late because of a problem with the dessert she volunteered to bring. I wonder what went wrong?"

"I guess even a great cook has a crisis now and then," Sam said. "I sure do, but I'm still pretty much a beginner."

My doorbell rang.

"I'll get it," Cleo said.

Soon Sam, Cleo, Alice, Doug, Zeke, and I were all seated at my dining table. Since I didn't own a coffeepot, Cleo had brought down hers and made a pot. I poured drinks, including tea for me and soda for Zeke, and Sam brought in plates.

Bella rounded the table, stopping at each person for attention, then took the doggy treat I handed her over to the corner and lay down, munching and looking up at us occasionally as if to reassure herself that all her people were here, and all were safe.

"What did you make, Alice?" Zeke eyed the plastic cake carrier.

"And what was your cooking crisis?" Sam asked. "After the way I burned some béchamel sauce last week, I'd kind of like to hear that another cook had issues."

Doug shook his head at Sam. "Sorry to break it to you, but if it wasn't for me, Alice wouldn't have had any problems with her cake. She might have made a few questionable recipes when we were first married"—he and Alice exchanged grins—"but these days, everything she cooks turns out great."

Pretty much what I'd expect. The woman was so on the ball.

Alice's cheeks grew slightly pink. "I made banana cake with cream cheese frosting. As for the crisis, I've been getting up early every weekday, studying a prep book for the ACT. The university said I don't have to take the exam because of my age, but I want to be on the same level as the rest of the freshmen. Since I'm getting up early, I usually eat breakfast before Doug gets up these days."

"Which is why she didn't know that I'd been eating the cream cheese she bought to use in frosting the next time she made a cake," Doug admitted.

"It did slow me down a little, but Doug ran to the store for me." Alice lifted the lid of the cake carrier, revealing a two-layer cake covered in beautiful frosting scallops and swirls.

There was a collective murmur of appreciation, and Zeke immediately handed his plate to Alice.

She sliced an extra-big piece for him, then served the rest of us.

Once a plate was passed to me, I cut off a large bite, making sure to get the perfect ratio of cake to frosting, and I popped it in my mouth. The cake was dense and rich and full of banana flavor. The cream cheese frosting was simply decadent, and the combination of the two was perfect.

For a long moment, there was no conversation, simply the sound of forks clinking against plates and the occasional "Mmmm."

"This cake is fantastic, Alice," I said. "And I'm so proud of you for going back to college."

"I haven't done it yet," she said. "I've started thinking of how I'll scale back some of my volunteering—not at the museum, of course—but I haven't even registered for classes."

"I'm sure you'll do well at Grove University," Sam said.

Alice brushed his comment aside and looked over at Cleo. "Did I hear you're going out with the new pediatrician in town?"

"Next Friday." Cleo wiped some frosting off her face. "My mom knows his aunt, and she's bound and determined that I get over Bryce."

Alice and I exchanged glances, and I could tell that she, like me, thought Cleo's mom had the right idea.

Cleo looked pointedly at one of us, then the other. "Yeah, I heard Bryce is back together with Darcy. But this new guy seems pretty cool."

"I hope you have a wonderful time next Friday," Alice said and then she turned to me. "Libby, you've got to explain how you figured out that Nick was having an affair with Brittany. I think, if I'd seen that drawing of a ring, I would have assumed it was something he was making on a commission for two other people."

Everyone at the table turned to me.

"Well, the first clue was the night Brittany died." I took a sip of my hot tea. "I stereotypically thought Nick seemed upset because he was an artist and had a sensitive temperament. In truth, he was probably barely holding it together because he realized he'd murdered the woman he loved."

"I can only imagine how he felt." Doug looked over at Alice.

"I didn't see it at the time," I said. "But when I thought about it later, it was obvious that he cared for Brittany."

"And they did both live in Nashville," Sam said. "And were very close to the same age."

I nodded and continued. "Plus, you found a really valuable clue, Zeke, when you noticed that Brittany's social media posts became more positive right after Christmas." I gestured to Sam. "Right about the same time you said Nick's business showed signs that he had gotten an investor. It occurred to me that if they got together, she might have been his new patron."

Alice's eyes narrowed. "So there was a connection with the timing. But Nick tried to throw suspicion off on Emmett, didn't he? With the way he told you that the police needed to focus on people who knew about science."

"That was sneaky." Zeke set his fork on his plate, which was already empty. "Instead of saying, 'Hey, I think Emmett is the killer,' he made a comment that seemed offhand but was actually intentional, meant to make us suspect Emmett because he was a research chemist. And Nick must have planted the poison in Emmett's room too."

"Nick was sneaky," I agreed. "Except for throwing that drawing away in the trash. If he'd been smart enough to burn it, I might never have figured it out."

Zeke leaned forward, both elbows on the table. "You did one thing that surprised me, though, Libby, when you yelled 'Fire.' Isn't it against the law to yell 'Fire' if there's no fire?"

"Ahh, the old 'can't yell fire in a crowded theater' thing, right?" Doug asked.

"Yeah," Zeke said.

"Actually," Doug said. "It's not illegal, although it's probably a bad idea."

Alice rested her chin on her hand. "You know, I think what you did really was a good idea at the time, Libby. You needed Leah to come downstairs. If you'd yelled 'Help,' she didn't strike me as the kind of person who would necessarily respond. And you didn't pull the fire alarm."

I bit my lip. I thought I'd been clever, but now it seemed like I'd made a big mistake. "I guess someone could have heard me yell and pulled it, though. And then the fire truck might have come to the bed-and-breakfast instead of somewhere it was really needed."

"Hey, don't forget that you stopped someone who had killed one person and tried to kill another." Sam said. "Besides, I'm just thankful that you and Cleo and Bella escaped unharmed." He reached over, squeezed my hand, and gave me a long look. "I've got another question. Where did Nick get a gun? Did he pack both cyanide and a gun to bring to Dogwood Springs?"

"Detective Harper said he bought the gun here," I said. "The local gun shop remembers him coming in the day after Brittany died. Nick admitted that once he bought it, he started carrying it with him everywhere he went."

We all sat silent a moment, and I wondered how many of Nick's actions had been spurred by his grief.

Cleo's forehead scrunched up. "I really thought Heather was the killer."

"I did too, but once I saw that drawing and thought about everything in light of a relationship between Nick and Brittany, it all made sense."

Sam looked over at me. "But after Brittany was dead,

why did Nick try to kill his dad by pushing him down the stairs?"

"He's not saying, but Detective Harper and I have a couple of theories." I took another sip of my tea. "Detective Harper thinks that when Brittany died and Nick no longer had her as his patron, he killed his dad to get his inheritance to fund his gallery." I shrugged. "That might be it, but I think after Brittany was dead, he resented his dad because Cordell had more time with Brittany."

"You know," Alice said. "It could also be that in some weird way, he wanted to blame Cordell for letting Brittany end up with the poisoned drink. If Nick could somehow convince himself that Brittany's death was partly Cordell's fault, it might make his own guilt easier to live with."

"That kind of makes sense," Cleo said. "But why not shoot Cordell, if he'd gone to the trouble of buying a gun? Why push him down the stairs?"

I sat back and thought for a moment. "You know, if Alice is right, and Nick was struggling with his guilt, after he bought the gun, he might not have thought he could go through with shooting his dad. If he pushed his dad down the stairs, maybe in his mind, it could sort of be an accident."

Doug rubbed the back of his neck. "I'm not sure I'd see it that way if I was Cordell."

"Me either," Zeke said.

I tipped my head in acknowledgement. "From what Rodney told me today at work, Cordell isn't pressing charges against Nick for the incident on the stairs, but he's writing him out of his will, and he told Nick that he's on his own for hiring a lawyer for Brittany's murder. Plus, Cordell plans to add something to his will so that if he dies in suspicious circumstances, none of his heirs gets a penny."

Doug rested both hands on the table. "Sounds smart to me. It would be hard to trust your family after a week like he's had."

"Except for Paula," I said. "Apparently, Cordell still trusts her. She's going to Nashville with him to supervise the nursing staff that will take care of him during his recovery. Rodney says with the way they're getting along now, he wouldn't be shocked if the two of them ended up getting remarried. As long as Paula doesn't have to go to big events with Cordell, Rodney thinks they would be happy."

"They do have a lot of history," Alice said. "And they were together before Cordell made his money, which probably makes it easier for him to trust that she's not after his fortune." She looked over at me. "Don't forget to tell them what Cordell said about the museum."

"Oh, I haven't forgotten, not for a moment." I sat up taller. "Cordell is making all the donations to organizations in town that he originally planned, so the museum will be able to get the elevator. Plus, as a thank you to us and especially to Bella, since attendance at the museum dropped after the murder, he's going to task some of his company's marketing team with helping the museum get back on track."

"Think of it," Alice said. "Libby and Imani do a wonderful job with marketing, but their time is limited, and the museum doesn't have the budget for things like professional graphic design."

"It's going to be amazing," I said. "When the elevator is in, we'll have that additional exhibit space in the big room on the second floor, and once everyone knows that the murderer has been caught and we get the marketing help, we should have lots more visitors. It's been a tricky couple of weeks, but the museum is going to end up fine."

"Thanks to you." Alice raised her coffee mug. "To Libby, an amazing museum director, a brilliant sleuth, and a wonderful friend."

"Hear, hear!" Cleo said.

"Hush." Heat crept across my cheeks, and I waved their praise aside. "It's you guys who are wonderful. You and Bella." I let out a heartfelt sigh. "I'm so glad I moved here."

I loved the little town of Dogwood Springs, and I knew without question that it was the place where I wanted to spend the rest of my life, here with my friends.

They were each so dear to me and did so much to make my life wonderful. Cleo, Alice, Zeke, and even Doug, who I didn't know quite as well, were more than just my friends, they were my family.

Over in the corner of the room, Bella let out a soft snore.

I chuckled. I couldn't forget Bella. She was such an amazing dog. Full of love, ready to cheer me up when I was blue, and incredibly smart. If it hadn't been for her, we might never have solved the case.

And Sam... I caught his eye. Well, Sam held his own special place in my heart.

"Thank you." Emotion welled in my throat, and I had to stop for a moment. "I never could have figured out that Nick was the killer without you. The six of us"—I glanced at Bella—"oops, the *seven* of us are an amazing team."

"I wonder if there will be any more murders in Dogwood Springs." Zeke slid his plate over to Alice, who served him a second slice of cake.

"I wouldn't think so. These past few months must have been a fluke." I folded my napkin and set it on the table. "But if there is more trouble in town, and if Detective Harper doesn't find the culprit right away, I bet we can figure it out."

Alice raised her mug again, and together we toasted our success.

Epilogue

Five days later

"BELLA, are you ready to spend the evening with Sam?" I pulled the passenger-side door open wider.

Bella needed no further encouragement. She leapt out of the car, did a lap around Sam's huge front yard, and raced to his front door, arriving on the porch just as I rang the bell.

But Sam didn't answer.

I dug my phone out of my purse. It was Saturday night, and I was sure I had the right time for when he'd invited me to dinner. Had he texted to say he'd been called away, and I'd missed it?

Nope. No messages. I sent a text asking if everything was okay.

Suddenly, I heard footsteps, and the door swung wide open.

"Libby! I'm sorry. I was shoving all the dishes in the dishwasher and didn't realize you'd arrived." He waved Bella and me inside. "Please, come in."

The two of us walked through the front door of Ashlington. When I was a child, simply stepping through that door to visit my grandparents filled my chest with bubbles of happiness. Now, as an adult visiting Sam, the feeling was almost exactly the same.

Bella wriggled past me and looked up at Sam with love —and a strong expectation of attention.

"Awww, Bella, you are such a good girl. I'm very glad to see you." Sam bent down, whispered to her how beautiful she was, and petted her.

She wagged her tail and rested her head against his leg.

I let out a long sigh. They were just so cute together.

After a moment, Sam stood up, took my coat, and wrapped my hands in his. "I'm glad to see you as well." His dark eyes shone, and he gently squeezed my fingers. "I really hope you enjoy the meal I've made. I think I finally mastered making béchamel sauce."

A swirl of happiness wrapped around my heart. Sam made me feel treasured. With every kindness and every special moment of attention from him, the pain of my divorce grew dimmer.

"What are we having?" I asked as I wandered into the kitchen and inhaled the aromas of beef, onions, garlic, and tomatoes. "It smells fantastic."

"I picked up bread from the Dogwood Springs Bakery, I used store-bought refrigerated pasta, and I bought some

Minnesota's Pride ice cream to go with our dessert, but everything else I made myself." Sam's voice rang with pride. "Caesar salad with homemade dressing, cannelloni filled with beef, pork, and ricotta and covered in red sauce and béchamel, and homemade shortbread cookies."

"Oh, wow! My mouth is already watering."

"I know your favorite is Mexican, but we just had that. Then I remembered how much you enjoyed the food at La Villetta, so I figured Italian would be a good choice."

I nodded, then noticed the pile of dishes to be hand-washed that overflowed the sink and covered my face with one hand to hide my grin. Sam was, deep down, a bit of a slob. His attempts to tidy before I came over always charmed me.

I peeked at the timer on the oven. "Only five more minutes to wait?"

"Is that all?" Sam checked the timer. "I'd better take care of a couple of things."

I filled water glasses and opened a bottle of red wine while he put the salad on the table and brought the bread out of the lower oven, where it had been warming.

Soon I was seated near one end of the long table in his dining room, a table that could easily seat twelve. But Sam had sectioned off our end of the table with a trio of vases of tulips, a thick, cream-colored candle burned between us, and instrumental jazz played softly on some hidden stereo system. The room, which might have seemed large and impersonal, felt intimate and romantic.

Sam served us each a plate of cannelloni and sat down across from me. "Please, give it a try."

I took a bite. A symphony of tastes swirled on my tongue, and my mouth spread into a wide smile.

He leaned in. "You like it?"

"It's delicious!" I took another bite. The pasta was tender, the meat-and-cheese filling was creamy and rich with flavor, and the red sauce and cream sauce blended in a divine combination.

He sampled the pasta, and his eyes narrowed, then relaxed. "I think I got it. Thickening the béchamel without burning it was the hardest part."

I dipped my fork into the top of the pasta, coating it with only béchamel sauce, and tasted it. "It's perfect."

Sam beamed. "Quite a couple of weeks we've had, figuring out who killed Brittany and learning that Ivy didn't die in a bank robbery in 1905."

"I'd say so." I took a sip of my wine. "We haven't completely figured out Ivy's mystery though. I really want to know where she ended up after she left Dogwood Springs."

Sam cut a bite of cannelloni with his fork. "It would be nice to find her descendants, wouldn't it?"

I nodded. "We can try searching for women named Ivy in Missouri in the 1910 census, but we don't know that she stayed in Missouri." I thought for a moment. "Social media helped us before. If we put together a picture of her with the clues we have, and I share it through social media with every museum professional I know, and ask them to share it as well, we might have a chance at figuring out where she went."

Sam ran a hand over the back of his neck. "I hate to say this, but it seems unlikely."

"I know. But someone might recognize her from an old photograph that was taken wherever she moved to."

"Possibly. If anyone is going to figure it out, Libby, you're definitely the person to do so. You're really good at connecting clues."

"As long as I have you and the rest of our friends to help me, it's easy."

Bella trotted over and looked up at me.

"And you too, of course, Bella." I gave her a pat, and Sam and I continued eating.

After dinner, even though I was eager to taste the shortbread cookies, we decided to move to the living room and wait for dessert. I, for one, was stuffed full of pasta. "That was such a wonderful meal," I said as I sat beside Sam on the couch.

He laughed. "My former colleagues would be shocked."

"You didn't cook back in California?" I snuggled closer to Sam.

"Did I ever tell you how my company made most of its money? The app I created?"

"It was an app? I assumed it was something technical that I wouldn't understand."

He pulled out his phone from his back pocket and pointed to an icon on the screen.

I stared at him. "Dinner Zapp? You made Dinner Zapp,

one of those apps that lets you order takeout from any restaurant in town?"

"I did."

No wonder Sam was incredibly rich. "That app is huge. But it is rather ironic that now you're learning to be such a great cook."

"I know. But I think I realized what I want out of life, and it doesn't involve eating dinner at my desk. It's a lot more fun solving the mystery of what happened with Ivy and spending time with you." He gave me a long, lingering look.

My cheeks grew warm, and tingles shot through me.

How did I ever get so lucky as to be dating this man? A man who appreciated both history and a good mystery? A man who cooked me a fabulous dinner and even made my favorite dessert, shortbread cookies? A man who could have dated any woman in town?

I gazed up at him. "I'm so glad we both moved to Dogwood Springs."

"Me too." He slid his arms around my waist and gave me a look brimming with promise.

My heart filled.

One day, we'd figure out where Ivy had gone after she left Dogwood Springs.

And, although I wasn't yet ready to say it out loud, one day, I'd tell Sam what I'd finally admitted to myself.

That somehow, despite being a bit gun-shy after my divorce, I'd completely fallen in love with him.

Thank you for reading this book!

Are you ready to return to Dogwood Springs for another cozy mystery? Join Libby, Bella, and their friends in the next book in the series.

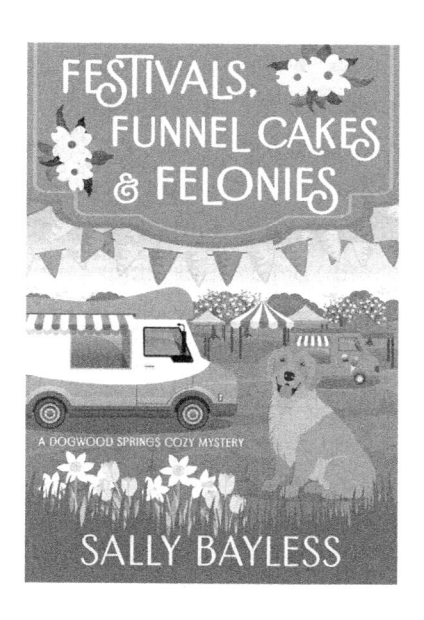

In the heart of a celebration, a dark secret festers.

The Dogwood Festival, held each year in the small town of Dogwood Springs, Missouri, is more than just a special event. It's a cozy haven of springtime charm, live music, and handmade crafts that draws tourists from all around. Libby Ballard, the dedicated director of the local history museum, is thrilled to be a first-time member of the festival steering committee.

As the festival approaches, the air buzzes with excitement.

But secrets simmer beneath the surface, and tragedy strikes when a fellow member of the steering committee is found murdered at the festival grounds.

When the police zero in on the wrong suspect and dismiss any connection to the festival, Libby realizes she must step in. With her loyal golden retriever by her side, Libby dives headfirst into a sea of suspects, each with their own motives, each a piece in a puzzle waiting to be solved.

Can Libby and Bella find their way through the labyrinth of lies and unmask the villain before another life is lost?

If you like a cozy mystery with an adorable dog, a warm circle of friends, and a dash of romance, you'll love *Festivals, Funnel Cakes & Felonies*.

Don't miss your free reader bonuses! Join Sally's cozy mystery newsletter to:

- download the prequel to the Dogwood Springs series, BED & BREAKFAST & BURGLARY, which is available only to newsletter subscribers
- read exclusive bonus content for every book, such as a scene in Bella's point of view

- learn about new releases, and more!

Visit Sally's website at www.sallybayless.com/free-mystery/ to join.

See all the books in the Dogwood Springs Cozy Mystery Series at www.sallybayless.com.

Acknowledgments

Before I wrote my first book, I imagined that an author sat at a computer, creating their stories, all alone. I have been delighted to find that, in the cozy mystery world, a writer can be surrounded and supported online by others who love the genre—both readers and fellow authors. I am so grateful to my cozy author friends and to all the readers who subscribe to my newsletter and connect with me on social media. You make writing cozies so much fun!

For this book, I am especially grateful to fellow author Tammy Doherty and to my wonderful beta readers: Betsy Anderson, Debbie Edwards, Ken Edwards, Barbara Hackel, Jennifer Hines-Bergmeier, Janice Huwe, Martha Long, Kim Lyons, Carrie Saunders, and Stephanie Smith. This book truly would not be the story it is today without your insightful comments.

Trish Long of Blossoming Pages Author Services edited this book and caught so many errors that might otherwise have slipped by. Thank you, Trish!

Donna Lynn Rogers of DLR Cover Design created the cover, which I absolutely love.

Last, but certainly not least, big thanks to my family—my husband, Dave, and our children, Michael and Laurel.

Thank you, Dave, for being the first person to give me feedback and for always being so encouraging. Thank you, Laurel, for beta reading this book. And thank you, Michael, for helping me when tech issues confound me!

If, in spite of help from all of these kind people, errors slipped by, please know that any mistakes are mine alone.

About the Author

After many years away, Sally Bayless lives in her hometown in the Missouri Ozarks. She's married and has two grown children. When not working on her next book, she enjoys reading, BBC mysteries, word puzzles, swimming, and shopping for cute shoes.

Made in the USA
Middletown, DE
17 September 2023